The Blind Years

Catherine Cookson was born in Tyne Dock, the illegitimate daughter of a poverty-stricken woman, Kate, whom she believed to be her older sister. She began work in service but eventually moved south to Hastings, where she met and married Tom Cookson, a local grammar-school master. At the age of forty she began writing about the lives of the working-class people with whom she had grown up, using the place of her birth as the background to many of her novels.

Although originally acclaimed as a regional writer – her novel *The Round Tower* won the Winifred Holtby award for the best regional novel of 1968 – her readership soon began to spread throughout the world. Her novels have been translated into more than a dozen languages and more than 50,000,000 copies of her books have been sold in Corgi alone. Fifteen of her novels have been made into successful television dramas, and more are planned.

Catherine Cookson's many bestselling novels established her as one of the most popular of contemporary women novelists. After receiving an OBE in 1985, Catherine Cookson was created a Dame of the British Empire in 1993. She was appointed an Honorary Fellow of St Hilda's College, Oxford in 1997. For many years she lived near Newcastle-upon-Tyne. She died shortly before her ninety-second birthday in June 1998.

'Catherine Cookson's novels are about hardship, the intractability of life and of individuals, the struggle first to survive and next to make sense of one's survival. Humour, toughness, resolution and generosity are Cookson virtues, in a world which she often depicts as cold and violent. Her novels are weighted and driven by her own early experiences of illegitimacy and poverty. This is what gives them power. In the specialised world of women's popular fiction, Cookson has created her own territory'
Helen Dunmore, *The Times*

BOOKS BY CATHERINE COOKSON

NOVELS

Kate Hannigan
The Fifteen Streets
Colour Blind
Maggie Rowan
Rooney
The Menagerie
Slinky Jane
Fanny McBride
Fenwick Houses
Heritage of Folly
The Garment
The Fen Tiger
The Blind Miller
House of Men
Hannah Massey
The Long Corridor
The Unbaited Trap
Katie Mulholland
The Round Tower
The Nice Bloke
The Glass Virgin
The Invitation
The Dwelling Place
Feathers in the Fire
Pure as the Lily
The Mallen Streak
The Mallen Girl
The Mallen Litter
The Invisible Cord
The Gambling Man
The Tide of Life
The Slow Awakening
The Iron Façade
The Girl
The Cinder Path
Miss Martha Mary Crawford
The Man Who Cried
Tilly Trotter
Tilly Trotter Wed
Tilly Trotter Widowed
The Whip
Hamilton
The Black Velvet Gown
Goodbye Hamilton
A Dinner of Herbs
Harold
The Moth
Bill Bailey
The Parson's Daughter
Bill Bailey's Lot
The Cultured Handmaiden
Bill Bailey's Daughter
The Harrogate Secret
The Black Candle
The Wingless Bird
The Gillyvors
My Beloved Son
The Rag Nymph
The House of Women
The Maltese Angel
The Year of the Virgins
The Golden Straw
Justice is a Woman
The Tinker's Girl
A Ruthless Need
The Obsession
The Upstart
The Branded Man
The Bonny Dawn
The Bondage of Love
The Desert Crop
The Lady on My Left
The Solace of Sin
Riley
The Blind Years
The Thursday Friend
A House Divided
Kate Hannigan's Girl

The Blind Years

A NOVEL

Catherine Cookson

CORGI BOOKS

THE BLIND YEARS
A CORGI BOOK : 0 552 14609 9

Originally published in Great Britain by Bantam Press,
a division of Transworld Publishers

PRINTING HISTORY
Bantam Press edition published 1998
Corgi edition published 2000

1 3 5 7 9 10 8 6 4 2

Set in 11½/14½pt Sabon by Falcon Oast Graphic Art

Corgi Books are published by Transworld Publishers,
61–63 Uxbridge Road, London W5 5SA,
a division of The Random House Group Ltd,
in Australia by Random House Australia (Pty) Ltd,
20 Alfred Street, Milsons Point, Sydney, NSW 2061, Australia,
in New Zealand Random House New Zealand Ltd,
18 Poland Road, Glenfield, Auckland 10, New Zealand
and in South Africa by Random House (Pty) Ltd,
Endulini, 5a Jubilee Road, Parktown 2193, South Africa.

Reproduced, printed and bound in Great Britain by
Mackays of Chatham plc, Chatham, Kent.

Youth is likened unto a field of weeds and tares
That harvests the blind years
And not until they are scythed low
Will new seed grow

Catherine Cookson, 1998

One

'Do you know, Bridget Gether, that I have been sitting beside you for the past five minutes and you haven't once looked at me?'

'I know you're there.'

'Well, that's something ... Sometimes you aren't aware of me, are you? You don't even remember what I look like, especially when you have a brush in your hand. What are you doing now?' He leant forward. 'That hill looks brown to me. It is brown; why do you paint it purple and orange?'

'Because that's how I see it. And ... and I do know what you look like, Laurence, even when I'm painting.' The young girl lowered her face towards the palette, still not looking at the man, and her shoulder-length auburn hair fell forward, covering her cheeks like a cloak. Her eyes, following her hand, lifted to the canvas set on the low easel on the grass at her feet, and her wide sensitive lips moved slowly as she added, 'I see you all the time . . . day, night, sunset, dawn.' She shivered slightly now as she felt his finger-tips moving through her hair to caress her neck.

'How do you see me?' Laurence Overmeer's voice became a thick whisper.

There was a pause before Bridget answered, with the trace of a laugh in her voice, 'As the tallest, broadest, handsomest man in the county.'

'What! Only in the county?'

'Well, perhaps in Northumberland and Cumberland too.'

'I should say so,' he said with a deep laugh as he pulled her round quickly on the camp stool, bringing from her a startled cry as the paint smeared across the picture. But she laughed too as he held her face between his hands, whilst he shook his head as his eyes scanned her features. And although it was quite some time before he spoke again she remained quiet, and then he said, 'What makes you so fascinating, Bridget? I'm always asking myself this, because you're no beauty, you know. Heart-shaped faces are out of fashion, and your skin's too brown to lay claim to the English rose type. Oh, yes, I grant you have a pair of eyes on you. Perhaps it is the eyes, as soft and grey as a doe's belly. But you're still no beauty, so what is it? Perhaps it's your aloofness, your dreamy aloofness that puts you just out of reach, makes a man want to grab at you. Is it that, Bridget?'

Bridget was no longer smiling. Her face looked almost sad as she said, 'I don't care what it is, Laurence, as long as it makes you love me.'

'I love you all right, and in a fortnight's time I'll show you just how much.'

Her head was drooping slowly forward when, with a jerk, she was pulled to her feet and lost within the circle of his strong arms, and when his lips pressed down on hers she responded hungrily for a moment, until with a sudden twist of her body she tried to withdraw from him.

He still held her close but their faces were apart, and now his expression looked puzzled and showed a trace of annoyance as he said, 'Why do you always do that, Bridget? Don't you like me kissing you?'

'Yes, of course I do, Laurence.'

'Then why?' Abruptly he broke the circle and his arms dropped to his sides. Bridget, stepping slowly backwards, looked straight ahead, her eyes on a level with his shoulders as she murmured, 'I don't know, Laurence. I don't want to.'

Then lifting her gaze to his face, she added simply, 'I do love you.'

'But you're afraid of me?'

'No, no, I'm not, Laurence, I'm not afraid of you. Why should I be? I've known you as long as I've known anyone.' She smiled. 'My first memory is of seeing you standing beside Grandma's chair and Grandma saying, "Stop stuffing yourself, Laurie. Hand over those sweets." '

'You've told me that before, but I don't believe you remember any such thing. I don't. And what's more, I never stuffed sweets.'

'Yes, you did. Grandma said you used to stuff until you were sick . . . you couldn't resist anything you liked.'

A stiff silence fell between them. The evening sun slanted their shadows, and so still were they that they merged with those of the trees that lay to the right of the small cedarwood house standing on a bank above the pool. The pool itself was merely a hollow in the rock plateau and was fed by a little burn that spluttered down the gully between the grey stone crags. The overflow from the pool tumbled over a long, partly wooded slope to the River Lune.

In the ten acres of the Overmeers' woods and gardens, the view from above the pool took pride of place. For beyond the sloping wood through which the burn flowed there lay the fells, with Mickle Fell rising like the father of them all, seemingly, from this distance, from the very bed of Lune Forest.

However, at this moment Bridget was not conscious of the beauty before her, for once again she was being assailed by a perplexing feeling. It had been brought about by her recalling the incident in Laurence's childhood; recalling it even when she knew it would annoy him. Why had she done so? The only reason she could think of was that some part of her, some small part of her, was not, as the French would say, *sympathique* towards him. It had the same meaning as when old Nancy, while she busied herself in the realm of the kitchen up at the house, would say when requested to give Kate, the housemaid, an order, 'You go an' tell her yersel, Miss Bridget, for I'm not kind with her the day.'

But why was this small part of her 'not kind' towards Laurence? for, as she said, she loved him. She had always loved him. But why was she asking the road she knew? She knew well enough why the small part of her was 'not kind'.

'Are you worrying about something, Bridget?' Laurence did not move towards her as he spoke.

'No. No, I have nothing to worry about.' She

turned and looked at him over her shoulder and their eyes held for a long moment before he said, 'There's no-one in my life now but you; d'you believe that?'

She didn't say, Yes, Laurence, for she was thinking, There's no-one in my life *now* but you, he had said. It was as if the *now* was fork-pronged and had pierced her in several different places, for all of a sudden she was alive with pain. He had not, as usual, said, There is no-one in my life but you, but had said, There is no-one in my life *now* but you.

'You do believe me?' He had moved towards her, and she answered simply, 'Yes, Laurence, I believe you.'

'Well, then, why are we so gloomy? Come on, let's get back: Mother has prepared one of her dinners supreme. You'd think I was going away for five years instead of five days. Will you miss me?' His broad chest was again blocking her gaze, but she looked up at him and, with deep feeling, said, 'Every minute you're away.'

'Kiss me, then.'

Her eyes widened slightly as she looked at his arms, now hanging straight by his sides.

'Put your arms around me and kiss me.'

Her head swayed and her long dark lashes quivered over her eyes before she brought out,

'But Laurence, I . . . I'll never get my arms about you.' But no part of his face answered the laughter that was now in her voice. His straight mouth was set, his nose, small for a man of his build, quivered slightly at its tip, and only a sliver of dark blue light penetrated from beneath his lowered lids.

Bridget leant forward and slowly pushed her arms around his neck, then, her eyes closed, she laid her lips on his. The pressure was gentle and it met with no response. After a moment, she was standing straight again, her eyes cast down; it was as if she had failed at some simple task and was deeply aware of it.

'I'm sorry, Laurence.'

'Sorry?' His voice was high and expressed open amusement. 'Why are you sorry? Come on, come on.' He thrust his hand under her chin and brought her face up to his. 'I asked you to kiss me and you kissed me. What more could I want? But come.' He took her arm now and turned her towards the easel. 'Get those messy things put away and let's to the house. If we're late for dinner we'll never hear the end of it.'

Obediently Bridget picked up the easel and palette and took them into the cedar hut, then returned for her paints. Back in the hut and standing behind the door, rubbing her hands with a turps-soaked rag, her head swung downwards sharply and she bit tightly on her lip. Why couldn't she have kissed him in the way he wanted? Why? He was angry, furious with her. Oh, she knew all the signs. And hadn't he said there was no-one in his life *now* but her? Well, if she wanted things to remain like that she had to stop being . . . what was the word? Diffident? Squeamish? Aloof? He said she was aloof, he had always said she was aloof. She didn't want to be aloof; the very sight of him always made her want to fling herself into his arms and press herself into him until she was lost.

His head came round the door: 'Come on, what are you playing at?'

'I'm just cleaning my hands.'

'You can wash them when you get in.'

'No, I must do it here; you know how Aunt Sarah loathes the smell of paint.'

As she stood washing her hands in the basin in the corner of the little single-roomed hut, Laurence's voice came to her from outside, calling, 'Oh, I forgot to tell you. Mother has had a letter from Grandma and she has decided to give you the tiara and the necklace for a wedding present.'

Bridget stopped soaping her hands and turned her head sharply to look towards the door as she exclaimed loudly, 'But I don't want them. Grandma promised them to Yvonne, and Yvonne thinks she is going to get them. She'll be so disappointed.'

'You take all you can get, my girl, especially from Grandma.'

'But I never wear jewellery, you know I don't; and Yvonne, being in America, would be tickled to death.'

'You never know when there'll be an occasion to wear a tiara. Anyway, she is going to give you them.'

'But she is giving me most of her silver and the Rembrandt and the Corot. I just can't take them.'

Bridget flung down the towel and hurried outside and repeated, 'I can't take them, Laurence; it wouldn't be fair to Yvonne.'

'Fair to Yvonne!' Laurence now scoffed. 'Yvonne is a cousin you've seen twice in your life and perhaps won't see again.'

'Of course I shall; you said we were going to America next year.'

'Yes, of course. Well, anyway, if Grandma has made up her mind that you ought to have the things there's little you can do about it. You know Grandma.'

As she hurried along silently by Laurence's

side, up through the rowan walk and into the wood, Bridget thought, Yes, I know Grandma. Who better? She had been practically brought up by her. To her, Grandma was mother, father and family, and she loved her dearly, but she was a stubborn old woman. She should know Bridget had no use for jewellery. Jewellery didn't attract her in the slightest. Besides, she had enough money of her own to buy all the jewellery she wanted, if indeed she wanted it. On the other hand, although Yvonne's people weren't needy, they were not in a position to buy their only daughter tiaras. Grandma was being perverse . . . she had bouts of perverseness. Aunt Sarah always said that Grandma was a female mule.

The thought of Laurence's mother brought a question to Bridget's mind. Aunt Sarah had gone to Chard in Somerset last week to stay with Grandma. Had she had anything to do with Grandma's decision to add to her already sumptuous wedding present? Yet she couldn't see Aunt Sarah carrying much weight with the old lady, for there had never been any affection between them. It all stemmed from Grandma taking for her first husband a widower by the name of Arnold Lacey. He was the owner of Balderstone House, and he had one child, named Sarah.

It was when Sarah was eight that the vivacious raven-haired county beauty, Hester Foley, became her stepmother. But it was only a year later to the very day that Sarah lost her father, and her stepmother lost her husband. It was on the day of the big hunt. In the evening they brought his body up, together with that of his horse, from the bottom of Pearson's Drop.

After a decent interval of three years, Sarah's stepmother had married Roland Gether. He wasn't of the county but was a rich industrialist, who believed in the maxim that where there was dirt there was money. So the family moved to Newcastle, although to the best end. Yet Balderstone House was not sold, for the simple reason it had been left to Sarah; it had been the birthplace of her mother.

From Hester Lacey's second marriage there were two sons, Arthur and Paul. They both married young and within a year of each other; and within another year their wives both gave birth to daughters. This was in the first year of the Second World War, and Arthur, fearful for the safety of his wife and child, sent them to America. Paul's wife refused to leave her husband and so set the seal on their fate, for it was during the Blitz that Paul and his wife, together with Roland Gether, his father, were

21

killed. Bridget, Paul's child, had been left with her grandmother, who at that time had been evacuated to Somerset, and she continued to live with her.

Years prior to this, Sarah Lacey had returned to the home of her birth, for at twenty-one she had come into the money that her father had left in trust for her. She opened up Balderstone House once more, and the house and its setting became the passion of her life. She was thirty-three when she met and married Vance Overmeer. Vance was six years her junior, tall, fair, charming and broke, but under Sarah's guidance he did not remain so for long. In the first year of her marriage she gave birth to a son, whom they called Laurence, and both inside and out he took after his father; there appeared nothing of Sarah in his make-up. Whether this vexed her or pleased her no-one knew, for no-one had as yet got beneath the skin of Sarah Overmeer.

Sarah Overmeer had the power to intimidate people, but she never had this effect on Bridget. Bridget had always liked her Aunt Sarah. She could not say that she understood her, but one didn't think about understanding Aunt Sarah. She was accepted for what she was, the unquestionable mistress of the house and the ruler of all therein, including the menfolk.

Bridget had always spent some part of her holidays at Balderstone; the main part she spent with her grandmother. From a convent school on the south coast, three times a year she had taken the train either up to Durham or to Somerset, according to which place it had been arranged she should visit first. As a child, she had always loved to be with her grandmother, but in her teens her conscience pricked her when, at the end of term, she found she wanted to be going north first, because then perhaps she would meet Laurence. Sometimes she considered herself lucky when the arrangement was made for her to go straight to Balderstone, until she arrived and experienced blank disappointment when she learnt that Laurence was away skiing or sailing; in later years he would be on business trips for the firm, for the name of Overmeer was now pushing hard in the textile business.

When she was eighteen it was decided she should go abroad for two years, one to be spent in Paris and the other in Germany. At this news she protested loudly. What was the use of being 'finished off'? She was not cut out to be a socialite. It was not that she didn't like people, she did. But parties and such entertainment had no attraction for her. She could dance, and liked it up to a point, but what she did like, what she

23

loved doing, was painting. All she wanted to do was to paint. But what was the use, they all asked, those in Somerset and those in Balderstone, who between them arranged her existence, 'You can paint as a hobby, but you don't need to strive at it, and you certainly don't need to earn your living by it.'

How many times had she wished that she did have to earn her living by painting, as then she would have stood firm and said, 'I am not going to waste two years.' But on the other hand, if there had been need for her to earn her living there would have been no talk of her finishing off, no opposition to hard work. Instinctively, she knew this.

All the way along the rowan walk and through the woods she became more and more aware of Laurence's displeasure, and it hurt her, yet at the same time she asked herself what did he expect her to do? What? What? The answer formed a vivid picture in her mind and brought the blood coursing through her body, and she became so hot she imagined that even her hair had darkened its shade.

Often when she asked questions of herself she received no reply. Her words and probings seemed to float away into the dreaminess that cloaked her. Yet at other times, like the moment just gone, she gave direct, almost lightning replies. This was when what she called 'the granny' part of her came to the fore. And she noted that, as she grew older, this part of her formed, more and more, a hard wedge in the calm remoteness of her character. Not only did it prompt her thoughts into vivid descriptive pictures, it also brought spurting from her tongue retorts that startled her hearers, and herself too. Still, these times were few and far between, and for the most part life, as it was lived between Balderstone House and her grandmother's out-sized cottage, flowed pleasantly around her; indeed, for the past six months, excitingly around her, for during these months she had become engaged to Laurence Overmeer.

How had she become engaged to him? She never really knew; there had been no tender lead-up to the declaration of love. It had begun one morning while she sat at the foot of her grandmother's bed opening the mail. Hester Gether had looked up over the edge of a letter she was reading, her eyes even at seventy-nine still holding the bright twinkle that had been with her from girlhood, a twinkle that at times could express much more than words, as it did at this particular moment when she said, 'Your Aunt Sarah says she would like you to go down, as there's a bit of a party being arranged. Laurence is bringing some friends over from Holland. She thinks you might enjoy yourself.'

The old lady had placed the letter slowly on the satin-quilted bedspread, then putting her hands on top of it palms downwards, she leaned forward from her pillows and said, 'Your Aunt Sarah is about to get you married off.'

'Who, me?'

'You sound like that funny cartoon man with his head over a wall . . . Who, me? Yes, you. She thinks you've been in your dream state long enough.'

'What do you think, Grandma?' Bridget had asked, returning the old lady's twinkle.

'I think that somewhere deep down you have a little bit of me in you, and you'll do the sensible thing.'

'And what's the sensible thing, Grandma?'

'Follow your heart.'

Grandma knew nothing about Bridget's heart having followed Laurence for years. Bridget had kept the state of her emotions from Grandma because she knew the old lady did not hold Laurence in very high esteem. Not that she had said anything openly about him, but there were telling silences when his name was mentioned, little wrinklings of the nose, a thrusting out of the lower lip, all expressing Grandma's opinion of her stepdaughter's son.

When Bridget arrived at Balderstone, surprisingly there had been no company, no young men from Holland, no party. It had fallen through, so Aunt Sarah said. But she didn't see any reason why she should stop Bridget coming as Laurence was at home and needed company.

Could the young men from Holland have been figments of Aunt Sarah's imagination? Not quite, because Laurence also explained that because the business end of the firm was in Holland, some special work had come up which needed the attention of two of his close friends. And a third young man had been taken ill. So there was no reason to think that the whole thing had been contrived to throw her and Laurence together.

Yet Hester Gether persisted in this theory when she heard the news that Laurence had proposed to Bridget.

Such was her fury, she threatened to make the journey at once to Balderstone; and so Sarah had advised Laurence to take Bridget down to her grandmother's immediately and prove – she smiled wryly as she said the words – that his intentions were honourable.

Bridget's interview with her grandmother was short, a matter of moments.

Why had she done it? asked Hester.

Because she loved him, Bridget had replied.

Since when? asked Hester.

Ever since she could remember, replied Bridget.

The old lady had sighed, dropped her head onto her hands and said, 'Send Laurence to me.'

Laurence spent more than a few minutes with the old lady. It was an hour to be exact, for Bridget timed him, anxiously watching the minutes tick away, wondering if he would come out of the room and say, Grandma has forbidden it. Yet at the back of her mind she knew that no-one could stop Laurence doing what he wanted to do, or take from him anything or anyone he wanted to have. Again she remembered what had been said at the time of the sweet incident, Stop stuffing, Laurence, stop stuffing . . .

When they passed through the rose garden and under the peacock-guarded yew hedge and came within sight of the house they still hadn't spoken.

Balderstone was an ugly house. Although it was almost impossible to imagine that anything built of natural stone quarried from the fells themselves could look ugly, Balderstone had achieved this. It resembled a huge box covered with a two-handled lid, the handles in this case being represented by groups of chimneys on the east and west sides of the slate roof. Even the lawns running up on all sides to its very walls did not soften it; and the windows, flat-fronted without eaves, and the main door, massive but without the tenderising touch of a porch, added to the bare, cold look of the whole.

If the stone had been draped with creepers the appearance of the house would have been altered but Sarah Overmeer did not like 'stuff' crawling over the house. She had some years before acquiesced to the construction of an iron balcony, to be attached to the south side and connecting the drawing-room and study windows, which had been converted into doors, but this was as far as she would go.

But whereas the façade of the house appeared and indeed was truly ugly, the gardens surrounding it were beautiful in layout and in the choice of shrubs. And beauty was evident too once you crossed the threshold and saw before you, rising from the far end of the large hall, the half-circular staircase with its wrought-iron balustrade. Wherever the eye turned it rested on shining antique pieces, and deeply upholstered chairs. The middle part of the hall floor was covered by an exquisitely worked Chinese carpet, its tones brilliant yet mellowing together, its butter-coloured base being picked up and repeated in the heavy brocade curtains at the windows.

The elegance of the hall was reproduced throughout the house, for Sarah Overmeer prided herself on never doing things by halves.

The hall was empty when they entered and Bridget, unable to bear Laurence's displeasure for another moment, turned to him and whispered, 'I'm sorry, Laurence.'

Laurence was arranging his tie in front of the slim mirror that stood between a pair of elegant side tables, and he jerked round to her, his whole manner and expression showing surprise as he said, 'Sorry? What are you talking about? What are you sorry for?'

Bridget swallowed and looked at her feet, then shook her head. This was Laurence at his worst. He could make you feel that you were the victim of your own imagination.

'Bridget sorry? Has our little Love-in-the-mist ever done anything in her life for which she would be sorry?' He was being cruelly playful and she couldn't bear it. Turning swiftly away from him, she was about to ascend the stairs when a door at the far end of the hall opened and Sarah Overmeer stood for a moment looking towards her.

Sarah was a tall woman, as dark as her son was fair, and of his height, but lean. She was wearing a blue velvet dress over which was a voluptuous bibbed white apron. She had her hands behind her back loosening the straps as she spoke. 'Dinner is in fifteen minutes and neither of you ready.' She turned from them and took a few steps towards an oak cupboard and, opening the door, she hung up the apron.

Sarah Overmeer was known in the countryside around for many things, not least for the quality of the food that was placed on her table. This was brought about by her vigilance in the kitchen. There was a story told about her and the cook she had engaged when she married Vance Overmeer. The cook had objected to her constant supervision in the kitchen – prying, she had called it – and had stated openly that no lady of her acquaintance would ever dream of demeaning herself by pottering in the kitchen. Ladies gave the orders and left the rest to the person they paid to carry them out. The story goes that Sarah ran the cook out of the kitchen by her neck. Whether or not this was true, the woman and her belongings were driven the five miles to the station to catch the midday train to wherever she was going.

There followed a number of other quick

dismissals, then in the town of Middleton, practically on the doorstep, she found Arthur MacKay and his wife Nancy, and she trained them both, MacKay as butler, and Nancy as cook. The household had run on oiled wheels ever since; at least the domestic side of it.

When Sarah reached her son she followed his gaze, to see Bridget disappearing around the corner of the upper balcony. Then turning from him and moving slowly in the direction of the dining-room she whispered, 'What's the matter?'

'Nothing.'

Pausing, she looked over her shoulder for a brief moment before going on again.

Laurence, standing where his mother had left him, clenched one fist tightly, then quietly thumped it into the palm of his other hand before striding across the hall in the direction of the study. Once inside he made for a drinks cabinet and took out a tray on which stood a bottle of whisky and a syphon, together with glasses. He poured himself out a stiff drink. Then, his eyes dropping to a large day calendar on the desk, he muttered, 'The fourteenth. Only the fourteenth. Fifteen more days, and what then?' Throwing off the whisky in one gulp he patted his mouth dry with his handkerchief, and his eyes held no doubt or speculative expression as he said to himself, 'It'll be my way; she's had her chance. If she won't bend she'll have to be broken, and the sooner the better.'

'Our little Love-in-a-mist.' Bridget repeated the phrase to herself as she reached the top of the stairs. Before, whenever Laurence used this phrase, it had held a note of endearment, indicative of the ethereal delicacy of her character, but as he had said it a moment ago his tone had held nothing but bitterness and thinly veiled anger.

Oh, she didn't want to upset him; why couldn't she act as he expected her to?

'And she's going past without even saying, "You're still alive, then."' The voice, coming from an open door to the left of her across the wide landing, cut off her recriminating thoughts and brought her round to face a man standing in the doorway in his dressing-gown.

'Oh, John, I'm sorry. I was going to look in when I had changed.' She hurried towards him. 'It'll take me only five minutes, ten at the most. How're you feeling?'

'Fine, fine . . . except for my legs, my head and my stomach; but the rest of me's fine.'

Bridget stood looking up at the man before her and laughed.

John MacDonald was as tall as Laurence, and

perhaps if his large bones had been covered as amply, he would have looked as big, but even under the dressing-gown his angular frame seemed to be fleshless. His face, too, looked bony, and this tended to give an overall sternness to his expression. Yet the sternness was relieved by a pair of deepset brown eyes that, behind their scrutinising, had a touch of humour and depth of warmth.

'I can never understand doctors being ill; I always thought they had some magic formula that protected them,' she said, still laughing at him. She always wanted to smile or laugh, she found, when in this man's company; his brusque manner had never intimidated her.

'So did I. Strange, isn't it?' He nodded at her. 'And then to be caught out by common, ordinary flu! When I think of all those fish swimming, swimming, swimming, and laughing up their gills at me . . . Lord, it makes me fighting mad. And it has to happen on my holiday! I ask you, did you ever know such luck? And then' – he thrust his finger at her – 'stuck here all afternoon and not a soul to talk to me.'

'Oh, I'm sorry, John; I'll come in for a long chat after dinner.'

'You won't, thank you very much; we'll do our talking downstairs tonight. I'm coming down to dinner . . . I'm all ready.' He pulled the lapels of his dressing-gown apart.

'Oh good . . . good. Oh, I'm glad . . . I'll see you in a minute, then. I must dash.'

She flashed him a broad smile as she turned and ran along the wide landing to her room.

She hadn't time for a bath, so she washed quickly, and applied her scant make-up, then pulled over her slight, almost child-like figure a semi-evening gown of grey printed cotton, its deceptive simplicity hiding its expensive and exclusive line.

She felt better now; she always felt better for seeing John . . . John who seemed like a brother . . . almost a father. Oh, not a father! Laughing, she chided herself for such a thought. He, at thirty-five, her father? But he did seem to be so much older than his age. Her Aunt Sarah said John had been catapulted into manhood at the age of twelve when, in 1940, he had lost both his parents in a raid over London. It was then he had come to live in this house. From that time he had looked upon it as home, and had called Sarah and Vance Overmeer aunt and uncle, although there was no blood relationship between them, for Sarah had merely been his mother's schoolfriend.

However, Bridget never connected Balderstone

with John, for he rarely now, except on this
occasion when he had been taken ill on his way
to Scotland for a fishing holiday, stayed more
than a couple of days here. But she supposed this
was understandable, seeing that he practised in
London. And then, of course, things had been
rather strained between him and Aunt Sarah
since his marriage, to which she would allude as
'that shocking affair'.

The ringing bell brought her whirling round,
and she was about to dash from the room when
she stopped, and going to the cheval mirror, she
looked at herself appraisingly for a moment. It
was as Laurence had said, she wasn't beautiful.
But he had also said she had 'something'.
She put her head on one side. What was it? She
couldn't see it, she couldn't feel it, but whatever
it was she prayed – she actually joined her hands
together – oh, she prayed it would hold
Laurence all his life.

She did not rush out of the room and run
across the landing and down the stairs as she
was wont to do when the last bell summoned;
instead, walking quietly, even sedately, she
descended to the hall, there to see Laurence and
John walking into the dining-room and to note
with amazement that they were laughing
together.

The sight actually halted her steps and brought to her body a feeling of warmth. How long was it since she had heard these two men joined in laughter? Not for many years. She hadn't realised until this moment how deeply she had been affected over the years by their feelings towards each other. Nor had she, until this very minute, identified the emotion that induced aloofness into the one and brought forth sarcasm from the other, as hate. But now they were actually laughing together, and as she neared the dining-room she gauged that their merriment was evoked by all the fish that were 'laughing up their gills' at John.

Of a sudden she felt so happy that she had the childish desire to jump, just to jump . . . up and down, up and down. She said to herself, Don't be so ridiculous, Bridget Gether, you're crazy.

As they turned towards her she knew that her face was alight, and after glancing at John she let the light shine fully on Laurence. And in it was a promise: she would love him as he wanted her to, she would, she would.

The meal in the long, high dining-room neared its end. It had not been the usual jocular affair with quips passing between Laurence and his father and punctuated by some witty shaft from

Sarah. Bridget had always liked meal times at Balderstone. It was at this table, and not in Germany or France, that she had become aware of good food ... and wine. Given more to listening than to talking, it was rarely that she monopolised the conversation, but there were times when she held them all with her brilliant bouts of mimicry. Only last evening she had given them a picture of the French family with whom she had lived, particularly the uncle who never came in sober. It was after the meal that Laurence had said laughingly, 'It must be the wine. You're only talkative at the table; I'll see that you spend most of your time eating ... and drinking after we are married.'

But this evening it was Vance Overmeer who had done most of the talking, and in the form of a vitriolic tirade against their nearest neighbour, Henry Dickenson. And the attack had had its effect on John who, as a young boy, and man, had maintained a friendly association with the Dickenson family.

There had been nothing in the nature of a feud between the Dickensons and the Overmeers – Vance Overmeer would have considered such a suggestion out of place; Henry Dickenson was a small farmer and as such was not to be considered on an equal standing with the owners of

Balderstone. Henry Dickenson had always been looked upon as someone a mere cut above a farm labourer. On the other hand, Henry Dickenson had always considered 'the Dutchman' an intruder and an upstart.

Henry Dickenson's father and grandfather had farmed the same acres of land when Sarah Overmeer's parents and grandparents had occupied the gaunt stone house at the head of the valley; then the house had not been surrounded by beautiful gardens but by fields, and should the sheep bounce over the low drystone-walled boundary, what did it matter? It hadn't mattered until Sarah had married Vance Overmeer and the Dutchman had brought the gardens down to the extent of the boundary and demanded that Henry Dickenson see that the partition between their lands was such that his sheep and cattle did not stray.

But every so often the farmer's cattle broke through into the gardens, and when this happened they brought, frothing up, feelings which by now affected Vance Overmeer in waves of fury. Vance had, this evening, been late for dinner, and as Sarah had exclaimed, 'I wonder what's keeping him,' Bridget could have replied, He's likely at the Dickensons. But she didn't. She remembered earlier in the day, from her high plateau near the pool, spotting the figure of Bruce, Henry Dickenson's only son, herding scurrying dots through a gap in the faint cream line which was the wall. And at the time she had thought, Poor Bruce, I hope he gets it fixed before Uncle sees it.

Unlike John, Bridget had always been able to keep to herself her sympathy for the Dickensons, both father and son. Unless, as tonight, the situation was forced upon her notice, she did not think much about her uncle's reaction towards his neighbour, but when as now she did, she considered it a pity that her uncle and Laurence, and also her Aunt Sarah, didn't know the Dickensons better, for if they did, she felt sure all this bickering over fences and walls would stop. The Dickensons were very pleasant people, especially Bruce. Bruce was very nice. She had a memory of a time, a secret time when she and Bruce had adventured together. It was a faint memory now and she did nothing to stir it.

Bridget was about to lift the glass of wine from the mat resting on the polished table when it almost sprang from her hand as Vance Overmeer struck the edge of the table with his closed fist and exclaimed, 'I won't stand any more of this! I'll take him to court.'

'Don't be silly, Vance. Finish your pudding.'

It was as if Sarah Overmeer was chastising a child, and like a child, the big, fair, heavy-jowled man moved his body within the carved hide-seated chair and became silent.

Bridget, spooning up the last of the egg custard and wine-soaked pears, wondered what would happen if she ever spoke to Laurence like that. The proposition was so outrageous that she almost spluttered on her food but managed to change the splutter into a discreet cough. Then Sarah spoke again. She looked down the length of the table and, addressing her husband, said, 'You know there's always been a question of who is responsible for the south boundary – it goes back as far as I can remember – but the Dickensons have always kept it in repair. If you had done as I suggested and had the wall built properly before the war, none of this would have happened.'

'It would have cost hundreds even then.'

'Far better that than have all this upheaval periodically.'

Now scraping his chair slightly away from the table, Laurence looked at his mother and said, 'If it went to court and were thrashed out we would know where we stood.'

'You'd know where you were all right; you wouldn't be standing, you'd be flat on your back.'

They were all looking at John now, and Bridget's heart contracted as she saw the tight line of his mouth, and she wanted to cry to him, Keep out of this, you'll only make matters worse. The laughter that had passed between the two men now seemed but a figment of her imagination.

'How d'you make that out?' Laurence's tone was deceptively cool.

'Because Aunt Sarah knows as well as Henry Dickenson does who is really responsible for the long wall.' John looked now towards Sarah Overmeer, whose face had an unusual tinge of colour about it.

She answered hastily, 'I know nothing of the kind, John. You are apt to let your feelings run away with you where the Dickensons are concerned. But anyway, we'll have no more talk about them or the wall or you'll find yourself with a temperature tonight, getting worked up over such trifles.'

As she ended her words with an airy movement of her hand John bowed his head, and Bridget, who was watching him from across the table, was amazed to see that his shoulders were shaking. His laughter made no sound, but when he lifted his head slightly and looked once again at Sarah Overmeer, Bridget was surprised, and not a little disturbed, by the expression on his face. As a prisoner might laugh at his jailer he was laughing at her aunt, and whatever his look conveyed it was evidently read by her, for again her colour deepened, to turn into an actual flush when, on a derisive note, he said 'You are an amazing woman, you know, Aunt Sarah.'

Whatever reply Sarah Overmeer would have made to this remark was checked by the opening of the door and MacKay entering the room.

MacKay did not look at all like the accepted idea of a butler. Had his trim black suit and white shirt been replaced by pit togs, a muffler and a cap, he would have presented the picture of a Durham miner, and it would have been a true picture for, before the slump in the Thirties, that's what MacKay had been. But now he was a proficient butler and served with almost fanatic devotion the woman who had given him and his wife security.

He closed the door discreetly behind him before approaching the table, and although he stood at his master's side it was towards his mistress he bent as he said, 'Mrs Crofton has called, sir.'

The announcement affected the company at the table in different ways, but only after a second of stiff silence, which they all shared.

Vance Overmeer coughed, then tapped his chest while looking towards his wife. Sarah Overmeer moved her six-strap pearl necklace slightly across her prominent collar bone. Laurence, with a quick thrust of his broad fingers through his hair, brought his hand round the back of his neck to rest on his lapel. John, for a brief moment, flashed his keen glance towards Laurence. Then, as if regretting the gesture, he bit on his lip and lowered his head again, but slowly now. Bridget's reaction was almost unnoticeable, except that her body gave a slight jerk. It was as if the pronged-fork of pain had entered her chest again.

And it was the mistress, not the master, who answered MacKay. 'Tell Mrs Crofton that I'll be with her in a moment. Ask her if she would kindly wait. Put her in the drawing-room.'

'Very good, madam.'

When the door had closed behind MacKay, Sarah, looking at Bridget and holding her eyes steadily, said, 'We shall go and join Mrs Crofton. You are finished?'

'Yes . . . yes, Aunt Sarah.'

As she rose from the table, Bridget looked towards Laurence. He was in the act of lifting the port bottle from the silver tray that stood to the right of his father, and so his face was turned from her. Nor did she catch John's glance, for although he was facing her his eyes were looking beyond her.

As Sarah Overmeer passed her husband she said calmly, 'There's no need to hurry.' And as if to illustrate this she walked slowly from the room, compelling Bridget to adapt her step to her own measured pace.

Over the years, Bridget had often thought whimsically to herself that she was only aware of having a heart when she looked at Laurence, for its beating would then echo loudly in her throat, and until lately she had imagined that the heart was the organ that expressed happiness. But of late she had learned that it had another function. It also expressed pain, and sadness, and bewilderment. And at this moment a mixture of all three was causing it to thump against her ribs, and she knew that if she looked down she would see the bodice of her gown jerking spasmodically.

'Good evening, Mrs Crofton. This is a surprise.'

Bridget was standing to the side of her aunt as she spoke, and she looked straight at the woman who had risen from the low couch that was placed facing the window. She was tall with hair nearly as dark as Sarah Overmeer's. She had a long pale-skinned face, a straight thin nose, wide full lips and two deep brown eyes whose sockets seemed to stretch beyond her cheek bones.

Bridget had not seen this woman more than half a dozen times, the first being three years ago. She was thirty-one then and had seemed old to her. Now at thirty-four she didn't look so old, but more beautiful than she had remembered her compared with their last meeting of almost a year ago.

The great eyes were on Bridget but only the mouth was smiling as Mrs Crofton said, 'I've brought a little something as a wedding present.' She pointed to a box standing near the couch head.

Although Bridget had in a way been 'finished', as the term is, she had never been trained in artifice or diplomacy, for there had seemed no need, and now she knew she lacked that support, she lacked the power to stretch her lips into a smile while keeping her feelings hidden behind the curtain of her eyes as Mrs Crofton was doing. She looked blankly towards the box and said, 'Thank you. It's very kind of you.'

'You must open it, Bridget.'

'Yes, Aunt Sarah.'

The string was merely tied in a bow and was quickly undone. Bridget pulled aside the wrapping to reveal an ordinary cardboard box. But when she opened it and looked down at the contents her eyes flicked towards Mrs Crofton again. Then one by one she took the pieces from the box and set them on the tray.

The present was a complete breakfast set for two, and in solid silver.

'It isn't new; in fact it's rather old. I thought . . .'

'But' – Bridget put in quickly, shaking her head the while – 'it's too much. It's very beautiful, but . . .' She turned and looked towards her aunt, and Sarah Overmeer, lifting her eyes from the antique six-piece Georgian breakfast set that she knew could not be bought, not even in an auction room, for two hundred guineas, turned to her visitor, saying, 'But how could you bear to part with it? Has it been in the family long?'

'No. No, not long, and I never use it . . . now.'

'Well, it's indeed kind of you, Mrs Crofton, isn't it, Bridget?'

'Yes' – again Bridget moved her head – 'it's much too kind. I feel I can't . . .' Whether she was about to add I can't accept it, or I can't thank you enough, was not quite clear for Sarah Overmeer exclaimed, 'I'm sure Laurence will be overjoyed; he has a taste for old silver. Do sit down, Mrs Crofton.' Sarah moved her hand in a small elegant gesture, indicating the couch again. Then, 'Would you like a glass of wine?' she asked.

'No, thank you. We dined early.'

'How is Mr Crofton? It must be . . . two, three years since I saw him last.'

'He's very well. He's in Glasgow at the present time on business.'

'And the children?'

'They're well, too. They returned to school last week.'

'Ah, yes, the autumn term. Laurence used to love the autumn term; it augured Christmas and lots of things to eat. I suppose your boys look at it in that light too?'

'One is a girl, Mrs Overmeer.'

'Ah yes, yes. I forgot. How old are they now?'

'Richard is ten and Mary eight.'

'Just the two?'

'I lost a baby last December.'

'Yes, how stupid of me. I remember. I'm so sorry.'

The younger woman and the older woman were looking at each other and Bridget was looking at them both. Sitting to the side of the table, her hand within an inch of the silver breakfast set, she stared at them, and she felt torn in two with pain, pain from the knowledge she would not face up to, and pain for this woman who was the cause of all her pain and who was now suffering under Aunt Sarah's cruelty. She began to lash herself for her own inadequacy in dealing with the matter. If only she were big enough, or strong-minded enough, to stand up and say, It's no business of yours, Aunt Sarah. If anyone's been hurt it's me, so stop your taunting. Grandma would have stood up; Grandma would have known what to say. Her self-denigration was startled and sent scurrying away by the drawing-room door opening abruptly and revealing Laurence about to enter the room. He was alone and paused for a second before moving forward slowly, as if he were feeling the weight of his body, and he looked directly at Mrs Crofton, and she, turning her head, returned his gaze.

But it was Sarah Overmeer who again took charge of the situation. 'Mrs Crofton has been very kind, Laurence,' she said. 'Look what she has brought as a wedding present.'

Still from her seat near the table, Bridget watched Laurence lift his eyes from Mrs Crofton and turn in the direction his mother was pointing. And now she saw him, for a brief moment, stripped of his cool composure. She watched his mouth drop into a tight line and his eyes screw into slits; and then his face was turned towards the couch again.

Mrs Crofton had risen to her feet and now stood not more than a couple of yards from him, her head almost on a level with his, and she was looking fully into his face as she said unsmilingly, 'I don't use it; I have no use for it now. I thought you might like it.'

With heightened pain-filled awareness, Bridget knew that both Laurence and Mrs Crofton were conscious only of themselves in this moment, and so vital and personally raw was the emotion filling this fraction of time that not even her Aunt Sarah had the power to break in on it.

It was snapped by Laurence himself. With a heave of his body he turned away from Mrs Crofton and came to Bridget's side. Putting his arm about her shoulders and pressing her body against his thigh, he asked, 'Do you like it?'

'It's beautiful.' She heard her own voice crackling slightly but she was surprised she had the power to speak at all.

'We'll have breakfast in bed.' He pressed her closer. 'We must have two special cups to go with it ... Wedgwood ... blue, thin, with scalloped sides, and we'll have China tea, strong China tea. What do you say to that?'

Bridget, resisting the pressure of his arm, straightened her body and pulled away from him. But it might have been her dead body she was relieving of his touch, for she knew as plainly as if he had told her, that, until a few months ago, he and Joyce Crofton had sat in bed together, and that she had poured strong China tea into blue Wedgwood cups with scalloped sides. And as they drank they had laughed. Oh yes, she felt sure they would have laughed. Yet such was her feeling for the evident agony of this woman, the agony that was being piled on top of the despair she was already carrying, the despair that had forced her to bring this telling wedding present, that she wanted to turn on this man whom she adored and cry, Stop it! Don't be so cruel. But she didn't; she couldn't lash herself to the point of retaliation of any sort for any reason . . . not against him. Yet she did do something.

To rise to her feet she had to press Laurence away from her, and this she did. Then walking firmly towards Mrs Crofton and looking up into her face, she said, 'Thank you, Mrs Crofton. I think it is a beautiful gift, and I shall always treasure it.'

The poise of the tall, beautiful woman was almost penetrated by the naiveness of the girl. Her chin quivered just slightly; her lower lip trembled before moving into its patterned smile; and then with chilling coolness, she said, 'I understand you are honeymooning on the Continent . . . travelling.'

'Yes.' Bridget smiled weakly.

'You must stay in Venice for a time. You mustn't miss Venice; you'll be enchanted. I know I was. I remember saying, as others have too, I wanted to die there. And who knows, I may do yet.' The lips moved into their set smile. 'Well, goodbye.' She did not make any reference to Bridget's future happiness, but turned abruptly from her towards Sarah Overmeer, saying with slow deliberation, 'Goodbye, Mrs Overmeer.'

In answer Sarah inclined her head before saying, 'I'll see you—' But she did not finish, for Laurence, moving quickly after Mrs Crofton as she made for the door, interjected in a tone that was almost a growl, 'I will see Mrs Crofton out.'

As Sarah's mouth sprang wide and her body jerked forward to countermand her son's statement, Bridget's small hand gripped her aunt's bare arm, and the older woman turned an indignant and startled glance on her. And her expression changed to one of open surprise when Bridget slowly shook her head.

This action of Bridget's, with its implied knowledge and forbearance, startled Sarah

Overmeer. This was not the reaction of an immature creature whose only interest in life was painting and whose eyes had always been blinded by her love for Laurence. For a moment she thought she saw before her, like a reflection in a mirror, the face of Grandma Gether, and the illusion frightened her. There must be no traits of Hester Gether in this girl or everyone in Balderstone would be damned, for the destiny of Balderstone lay in this dreamy, pliable girl's hands. Without her and what she stood for, Balderstone could go back to what it was forty years ago: a stark, stone effigy without warmth, inside or out, representing nothing but the ugliness of unimaginatively arranged stone. The thought was terrifying, for Balderstone was not only Sarah Overmeer's home and interest, it was her life and had replaced the natural passion which had never achieved full expression.

Bridget now loosened her hold and turned from her aunt, saying, 'I'm going upstairs, Aunt Sarah; I promised to have a talk with John.'

'You can't do that, Bridget; it's only eight o'clock and Laurence is off first thing in the morning. You must stay. Anyway, it isn't likely that John has gone up yet.'

Bridget turned again, and looking into the formidable countenance, she said quietly, 'In any case I would like to go to my room. And . . . and' – she paused before going on – 'I think that Laurence would prefer to be left alone tonight by everybody, Aunt Sarah.' She laid slight stress on 'everybody'.

Sarah Overmeer moistened her lips, then dabbed at them with a fragile handkerchief before whispering, 'You know about this, then . . . about the Crofton woman?'

Bridget blinked rapidly as she fought inwardly to suppress the urge to bring her knowledge into the open. Her answer sounded stilted and false as she said, 'I know nothing, Aunt Sarah; no-one has ever told me anything.'

'But you know?'

'I said I know nothing. I only feel things. Now, if you don't mind, I'll go upstairs. I'll leave through the balcony.'

As Sarah Overmeer watched Bridget leave the drawing-room she felt suddenly old and the feeling made her grope towards a chair and sit down, and again she used her handkerchief on her mouth, for now her upper lip was covered with beads of sweat, and the sweat was bred of fear. She must talk to the child. She must be candid . . . at least up to a point. If anything were to happen at this stage . . . The thought brought her to her feet. She must talk to

Laurence, no matter how mad he got. She turned to leave the drawing-room, then stopped . . . John. The name was audible. She wished he was out of the house. How soon would it be before he would go? Two, three days, a week. He wouldn't stay for the wedding, she was certain of that. Yes, she was certain of that. She must do her utmost to get him away as soon as possible: he was dangerous, as dangerous, in a way, as the Crofton woman.

Bridget had sat for some time at the window, looking into the slow northern twilight. The pain in her chest had spread all over her body, making her limbs feel heavy. She had the urge to fly down to the cedar hut and grab up her paints and lose herself, as she was capable of doing, in the transference of nature to the canvas. But even if it had been light enough she knew that that escape would, from now on, no longer help her, for in the well of her being the mists were clearing, and as they rose they were turning into vapour the dream world in which she had taken refuge during all these years; and soon she knew she would be face to face with her real self. The wedge in her make up that she had inherited from her grandmother was forcing its point into her mind, demanding that she face up to facts, to life as it was, not as she wanted it to be. But once she acknowledged its presence there would be no return to the vagueness, the aloofness, the protective screen against the reality of life.

When a knock came on the door she said, 'Come in', without turning her head. She knew who it was; not Laurence or John. Aunt Sarah had her own particular way of knocking on a door; it said, This is my door, I own it.

'You shouldn't sit in the dark, Bridget.'

'I like the dark.'

There was a pause while the older woman came and sat down next to her on the deep window sill.

'We must talk, Bridget.'

'Has Laurence gone out?' Bridget asked the question without turning her gaze from the window.

'Yes.'

'Has he taken Mrs Crofton home?'

'No! No!' The denial was emphatic. 'He's just gone, not more than five minutes ago. He took the dogs; he's just gone for a walk.'

Six miles divided the Crofton house from Balderstone, but what was six miles to two terriers and a man possessed? On the last thought Bridget turned herself around from the window seat and faced her aunt, and Sarah

Overmeer, putting out her hand and with unusual gentleness, murmured, 'It will be all right once you are married. Try and understand that.'

'Was it all right with you, Aunt Sarah?'

The question startled them both. An hour ago it would have been the last thing in the world she would have said to her aunt. She would have even disclaimed any knowledge of what the question implied, but now it had been asked, and she knew it was framed and formed on the memory of unfinished sentences, of guarded looks, of pithy enigmatic comments from Grandma; but most of all it was formed by the docility of Uncle Vance when dealing with his wife.

'How did you know that?'

Bridget shook her head. Even if she had wanted to she could not have explained the knowledge that had been garnered and hidden through the years.

Sarah Overmeer rose from the seat and began to pace the room, her hands joined tightly before her. She paced in silence for some moments, and then, seating herself once more, but with her face half-turned from Bridget now, she said, 'These things happen, and far better that they should happen before marriage than after.

Bridget' – she paused – 'if I thought you were going to have my kind of life with my son, as much as I want this marriage to take place, I wouldn't let you go through with it. You think me a hard woman.' She lifted her hand in a quick slapping movement to dispel any repudiation of this truth. 'Most people do. My hardness has been my sanity, my safeguard. Your uncle began his affairs shortly after Laurence was born. I was powerless against them. He is travelling most of the year, as you know. The one thing I was thankful for at first was that he always came back to me. Now I am thankful no longer. You reach a stage when you become sufficient unto yourself; you can suffer no more. If Vance now had his women all round the estate it wouldn't hurt me. The only thing that would hurt me would be if one of them crossed the threshold of this house.'

'Oh, Aunt Sarah.' Bridget was on her knees now, gripping the older woman's hands, and she said again, 'Oh, Aunt Sarah, I never knew, not that. Not how you felt. I'm sorry, I'm sorry I said anything. I wouldn't have hurt—'

'Sh! Sh! Don't upset yourself. I know you wouldn't hurt me, not knowingly.' Sarah Overmeer looked into Bridget's face. The conversation had taken an odd turn; perhaps it was just as well, for now she had the sympathy of this girl who, did she but know it, held the future of her beloved house and all those in it in her long slim hands. She said, softly now, 'What I feel is of no account; don't worry about me. I have other compensations, but you . . . We must talk about you and Laurence. You love him, don't you?'

'Yes, Aunt Sarah.'

'But you're afraid of him?'

'Yes, a little.' There was no need for subterfuge or evasion now.

'But do you like him?'

'Like him?' Bridget screwed up her eyes. 'Like him, Aunt Sarah? I don't understand.'

'No?' A gentle smile touched Sarah Overmeer's lips. 'No, it was a silly question to put to you. It's a question that no woman in love can answer. It is only after you are married that that question becomes important, and even then it may be years before you can understand it, but it is one of the fundamental aids to happiness with a man. You can love a man and hate him at the same time, but if you like the man, like his ways, his thinking, the little intimate habits that are his, if none of these gets on your nerves – in short, if you like him – then love can be a very joyous thing.'

Bridget bowed her head. Did she like Laurence? She hardly knew him. The answer startled her with its suddenness. But it was true; she hardly knew Laurence at all. She had loved him with a schoolgirl passion, with an adolescent passion, with the passion of a young girl who had never been in love with anyone else, who had never opened her eyes wide enough to see another man; but would she love him as a woman, and as he wanted her to love him . . . even before they were married? And after all this would she, as Aunt Sarah said, like him? To this last disturbing question she could give no answer. But Sarah Overmeer answered it for her.

'Once you are married,' she said again, 'everything will fall into place. Laurence will love you as he has never loved anyone else. You understand? He's big and you are small, at least small in comparison, and you will bring out the tenderness in him. It is all very well for people of the same stature to marry, but they become like combatants in a wrestling match. It is different when a woman is much smaller than a man. Look at me, Bridget . . . you understand what I am trying to tell you?'

When Bridget made no answer Sarah went on, 'You can have him eating out of your hand. You can make him your slave. These are platitudes but they are true. And you have got something in you, Bridget, some attraction that I never had, that few women have. It's not in your looks, and I don't know whether it's in your manner, your kind manner, or your voice, or the lifting of your eyebrows. Oh, I can't describe it, but it's an indefinable something; and you've got it. And you can hold him with it, I tell you. It's up to you. But look, Bridget . . . listen to me.' She now cupped Bridget's face between her hands, and staring down into it, she said, 'You must love him, live for him, and only him. You must be mother, wife and mistress to him. Do you follow me? Do you understand what I am saying, or have I to put it plainer?'

'I understand, Aunt Sarah.'

Bridget drew away from her aunt's hands, rose from her knees and walked to the window once again, where she stood gazing out on to the now dark night, and Sarah Overmeer, rising to her feet, her manner and tone reverting completely to normal, said briskly, 'Laurence has decided to go by a later train, the eleven-thirty from Durham. Your uncle will drive us up and we can see him off there. Then we can go on to Newcastle to do some shopping. Would you like that?'

'Yes, Aunt Sarah.'

'Good night, Bridget.'

'Good night, Aunt Sarah.'

After her aunt had left, Bridget still stood look-ing into the softly illuminated blackness of the night. One thing only seemed to have emerged from the emotional exchange that had passed between them and it was that no matter how much she wanted to marry Laurence or he her, his mother desired the match with an urgent passionate intensity.

She stood at the window, her eyes straining into the shadow beyond the edge of light from the drawing-room windows, until she became chilled, yet she didn't move away. She was wait-ing for Roy and Gip to come bounding into the light; she was waiting to hear Laurence's voice checking their pell-mell race into the house. Not until she actually began to shiver did she turn from the window and switch on the light.

As she took a wrap from the wardrobe she thought, He could have taken them in by the yard way. But he never took the dogs in by the yard way. The two Sealyhams were Sarah Overmeer's special pets and, being so, were privileged to use the front door, where just inside stood an oak box that held cloths with which to wipe their feet. If he had come the back way the dogs would have scampered round to the front door as a matter of routine.

To turn her thoughts away from the possibility of where Laurence might be at this moment she now went hastily from the room, down the wide landing and knocked at John's door. Before any response came to her knock she heard quick muffled movements within the room. Then his voice called, 'Yes? Yes? Who is it?'

'Me . . . Bridget. Are you in bed?'

'No, no. Not yet. Come in.'

When she opened the door and saw him sitting in his dressing-gown by the side of the open fire she paused as he hastily knotted a silk scarf about his neck.

'You were going to bed?' She crossed the room towards him.

'Well, yes, but I can leave it for a moment.'

'You look tired. You've been up too long.'

'I am a bit tired.'

'I won't stay then.'

His answer to this should have been, Nonsense, sit down! But he said nothing, and for the first time she could remember she felt embarrassed in his company, and knew without a shadow of doubt that he wanted her to go. He wanted rid of her.

It was as – with her colour rising – she was

63

about to turn from him that two oddities about his apparel jumped simultaneously to her notice: the first, that he was wearing his dressing-gown over his coat, the bulk of the sleeves giving evidence of this; the second, and more noticeable, was that he had changed his shoes. At dinner he had naturally worn black shoes with his dark suit; the shoes he was wearing now were heavy brown brogues.

Only just in time she stopped herself from exclaiming, You're not going out! You're not fit yet, and it's turned cold.

He had evidently been on the point of going out when she knocked. Suddenly she felt sad and slightly weary: everybody, even John, seemed to have separate and secret lives. Where could he be going at this time of night? Not just taking a walk: he wasn't fit for walks yet, and if his object had been as simple as that he wouldn't have tried to hide it from her, would he? But he needn't be going for a walk at all. He could be taking the car; perhaps he wanted to run down to the Stag in the village two miles away, and as Aunt Sarah didn't look with favour on any of the household frequenting the village pub he might have been going off on the quiet . . . But it would be difficult to make the car understand he needed to make his exit from the courtyard quietly. The cryptic thought brought a sigh from her and she said as offhandedly as she could, 'See you in the morning then.'

'Bridget.'

She looked at him over her shoulder.

'Come here.'

She turned obediently and went and stood before him. Taking her hand and looking into her eyes, he said, 'Don't think too badly of Mrs Crofton.'

'What!' She shook her head. 'W . . . what do you mean?'

'Come on now,' – he shook his head back at her – 'you don't have to put a face on things, not with me. You know that.'

'I . . . I don't want to talk about it, John.'

'You should. You should want to talk about it with somebody.'

'It's over and done with.'

As she bowed her head he asked, with a deep note of sadness in his voice, 'You love him very much?'

'I'm going to marry him.'

'That's got nothing to do with it. Do you love him?'

'Yes, yes, of course. You know I do. Why are you asking me?'

He gazed at her in silence for a moment before

saying, 'I just wanted to hear you say it and . . . and well, perhaps point out that what you see in him to love, others might do too, like . . . like Mrs Crofton . . . Now, now.' He gripped her hands. 'Don't get angry. Only feel a little sorry for her, for remember, you cannot help whom you love – it's like a disease, loving; it just hits you and you're finished; you go down under it . . . I know it, and you should know it, for as you say, you love him.'

'Oh, John.' She was about to cry; she was about to fall against him and cry her heart out. But no, no. That would be admitting there was something to cry about and there wasn't. No, there wasn't. All that was in the past, and, once they were married, as Aunt Sarah had said, everything would be all right. There would be nothing left of the past except the silver tea set. She turned swiftly away from him, saying now, 'I don't want to talk about it, John. Good night.'

Not until she was actually closing the door did his voice reach her. 'Good night, Bridget,' he said.

On the landing she hesitated, wondering again whether she should go downstairs and wait for Laurence, but the thought of sitting opposite her aunt and exchanging small-talk while both their minds would be on other things – or one other thing – diverted her steps towards her room again.

Once inside her room her mind turned to John and she began to speculate on the urgency that had made him get ready to go out, then try to hide from her the fact that he meant to go. Mrs Crofton? The name, ever present below a thin skin in her mind, burst through. John knew her. He had known her before Laurence. It was John himself who had introduced her to Laurence. John had at one period, and for a short time, worked with Mr Crofton, and when he made his flying visits to Balderstone he had sometimes gone over to the Crofton house. That's how it all had started. Had John been smitten too by the woman? The question came at her and set her mind racing backwards. There had been that one particular time when he had spent a week here resting and he had visited the Croftons quite often. It was just after this that he had suddenly got married. She had always felt that there was something odd about John's marriage. He had not told her he was going to be married and yet he had talked to her a lot that week. Down the garden, there to the side of the pond, they had sat, their legs hanging over the rock, watching the water rushing from the crevice and then lose momentum on its way to the river. Sitting dangerously, he had called it. It was just before the time she was going to France for a year. And he had held her hand in his and looked across the valley towards the fells, the while saying, 'When you get across the water they will try to drag you out of fairyland; they'll use a ram on the door. Don't open it, Bridget.' She had not replied, Oh, you are funny, John, for she had known what he meant.

The next week he had written to Aunt Sarah from London to say he was married.

It was during the following Christmas holidays that she learned more about the marriage. Aunt Sarah was still fuming with indignation. John had married a woman not only ten years his senior, but a one-time hospital sister who was addicted to drink and, much worse, drugs. John was a madman; she wiped her hands of him.

Bridget had cried at the news. Some part of her was torn asunder for John and his marriage, yet at the same time she understood what had made him do it. He had married not in blindness, but in compassion. Beneath his bluff exterior, John was all compassion.

A year ago she had dared to break her journey across London and knock on a paint-scarred door in a side street in the East End. The door held a brass plate which announced, 'Dr John

MacDonald, MD'. A woman with a coloured bib pinafore came to the door and said, 'Can't you read?' Then after a second glance at Bridget she asked, 'You wanting the doctor?' 'Yes,' Bridget had said ... she was a friend of Dr MacDonald.

Oh, then she'd better come in.

Bridget had been shown into a frowzy sitting-room. She was appalled at the shabbiness of it. She had forced herself to look at the woman and say, 'Are you Mrs MacDonald?', which brought a staccato howl in reply: 'Me! Mrs MacDonald? I hope not, me dear; she's been dead a month.'

John hadn't seemed too pleased to see her. He made no apology for the condition of the house and when she said to him, 'Why didn't you tell us about your wife?' he had answered bluntly, 'Now why should I? Would there have been anybody concerned down there? Relieved, oh yes, but not concerned.'

'I would have been,' she had said.

'That's nice to know,' he had answered, and then he had laughed an odd harsh laugh, the memory of which had remained with her for a long time, puzzling her.

But where did Mrs Crofton stand in John's scheme of things?

It was when, some ten minutes later, she was

going down the landing to the bathroom, that the tell-tale creaking of a door being slowly opened lifted her last steps into a scamper and brought her under cover of the archway that led into a recess and the bathroom itself. She hadn't a doubt but that it was John's door that was opening. A moment later she saw his tall muffled figure walking towards her, and panic gripped her. He would think she was spying on him. If she opened the bathroom door the noise would attract him, but if she remained still perhaps he wouldn't look her way. He was making for the back staircase. She closed her eyes. When she opened them he was gone.

The back staircase ended in a hall from which a passage ran to the kitchen and a door which led directly into the courtyard. The door naturally was locked at night. Had he a key? Or would someone downstairs let him in? But who? MacKay? No, MacKay would do nothing that his mistress did not know about. Nancy, his wife? Kate, the housemaid? No, not Kate. Kate had never cared for Mr John. Mr John never slapped her buttocks like Mr Laurence did . . . On this thought Bridget passed her hand tightly over her mouth as if the action would press it back into the knowledgeable depths whence it had sprung. She turned swiftly into the bathroom.

It had been a beastly day; she would be glad when tomorrow came ... But tomorrow Laurence was going away. This being so, one would have supposed that he might have wished to spend the evening with her, but no, he had taken the dogs for a long walk ... a long, long walk ... perhaps a six-mile walk.

Again she had the desire to cry, but again she checked it. She wished, oh she wished it was the twenty-ninth, because once she was married, as Aunt Sarah had said, everything would be all right.

Two

Just before the train was due in, Sarah Overmeer walked down the platform with her husband by her side, leaving Laurence and Bridget alone for the first time that day. Not for a moment had she allowed a private word to pass between them. If Laurence was aware of this, he had made no protest. It was as if he was blind to his mother's strategy or careless of it. Since greeting Bridget at breakfast with a nod of the head and the unusual enquiry as to how she had slept, he had not spoken to her. From breakfast until Ned Ryder, the outside man, had brought the car to the door, he had been closeted in the study with his father, and during the drive from Balderstone to Durham he had driven the car, his father seated beside him.

Now Laurence, looking straight at Bridget,

said, 'Do you want to ask me any questions?'

'No, Laurence.'

'You should.'

'I believe what you said to me by the pond last night.'

'What was that?'

'That there is no-one in your life but me.'

'Oh, that. Yes.'

'Is it true?'

He inclined his head slowly, then said, 'Yes, it's true.'

'Then nothing matters, does it, Laurence?'

He put out his hand and took hers, and now almost sadly, he said, 'You're sweet, Bridget, and trusting, and fascinating. Never change. Promise me you'll never change.'

There was a sudden bustle on the platform, a movement of people, and Sarah and Vance Overmeer were once again by their side.

'Goodbye, Father.'

'Goodbye, Mother.' Sarah's cheek was turned towards him.

And now he turned to Bridget again. Bending towards her, he kissed her lightly on the mouth. Then just before entering the carriage he covered them all with a smile as he said, 'This is the first time I've been seen off for only a five-day journey. It seems ominous to me.'

'Do as we arranged and there'll be nothing ominous about it.' Vance had moved forward and was looking at his son, and he added quietly, 'Do the best you can.'

Through the wide windows of the carriage Bridget watched Laurence being ushered to his place, and when he was seated the train began to move again and he turned and waved to them; then his eyes holding Bridget's, he put his fingers to his lips and blew her a kiss. It was such a light airy action that it sent a spurt of gaiety through her, and she answered it in a like manner.

She watched the train move away, then turned to find Sarah Overmeer smiling at her. And Bridget knew that her aunt was pleased. She would have gathered this much even if the older woman hadn't unbent to the extent of drawing her hand through her arm as they walked the short distance from the platform to the car.

And Sarah Overmeer's pleasure was confirmed on the journey from Durham to Newcastle, for from time to time she would turn her head and smile at Bridget, and each time the smile spoke of the secret that lay between them: the secret that concerned Laurence, who was like his father but who would be different once he was married.

And all through the shopping expedition and

all the way back to Balderstone Bridget confirmed in her mind Aunt Sarah's words: Once
you are married everything will be all right.

They arrived back in Balderstone at about
five-thirty, and after a cup of tea in the drawing-
room Sarah Overmeer said she was feeling a
little tired and would rest until dinner. What was
Bridget planning to do with herself?

'Go up and keep John company until dinner
time,' Bridget had answered; whereupon
MacKay, who was on his way out of the room,
stopped and said diffidently, 'Mr John is out,
Miss Bridget. He left the house about an hour
ago.'

'Oh, how stupid of him. It's quite damp out.
We'll have rain,' Sarah Overmeer put in quickly.
'If he's not careful he'll undo everything and find
himself in bed for days again.'

She sounded distinctly annoyed, and Bridget,
her head bent over her cup, wondered what her
aunt's reactions would have been if she had
known of John's leaving the house last night.

Now rising from her chair Sarah Overmeer
said, 'It wouldn't do you any harm to rest until
dinner either.'

'Rest!' Bridget's brows went up. 'All right,' – she
smiled – 'I'll rest while taking the dogs for a run.'

This brought an answering smile to the austere face. 'That's nice of you. They'll love that. I don't think they care much for their outings with Ryder: he's apt to take short cuts I think, with long rests between, and as they don't smoke they get bored, poor dears.'

Again they exchanged smiles, wider this time.

After running upstairs and changing into flat-heeled shoes and a wide-skirted dress, Bridget came down at the same pace, then called the dogs to her and set off.

At the end of the drive it was the dogs who decided the direction they would take. Pelting down the road to the right and heedless of Bridget calling them, they had almost disappeared from sight when, of one mind, they turned and raced back to her. And this was the pattern of the walk. On they would scramble, under gates, which she had to climb, across the river, jumping the stepping stones more sure-footedly than she could, over rocky, scree-studded fells, until they came within sight of the forest. Then at one point the dogs turned off to the left and made for a thick copse known as Marlow's Hollow. She had only once been through this particular copse and wasn't enamoured of it, for the ground was treacherous, being studded with bracken-covered pot holes. It was said that years ago a man called Marlow had started opencast mining on this spot, and when, through a lawsuit, he was prevented from carrying the work further, he shot, not only himself, but his family of three. They had found them in one of the holes. The story encouraged few visitors to the hollow, only those with little imagination. But as the Hollow lay near the far boundary of the Dickensons' land Bridget decided to circuit it, then take a short cut through the farm which would bring her to the wall – the dividing wall that was the cause of so much trouble – and so she would be home in time for dinner. Otherwise, were she to return by the way she had come, she would undoubtedly be late.

The dogs had disappeared into the copse and she did not call them; they evidently knew this way better than she.

This thought was in her mind when she came to the actual thicket and heard them barking excitedly. They hadn't barked up till now. She wondered if they had found something – a fox-hole perhaps. She was reluctant to enter the copse but she did, going in by what looked like a well-worn path: very likely Laurence or MacKay came this way often.

She was almost through the thicket when she

came upon the dogs, and the cause of their excitement seemed to jerk her heart into her throat.

Kneeling on the ground in a bracken-bedded hollow was Mrs Crofton. She had her arms about the dogs, her head straining back from their long-tongued kisses, and it was from this position that she saw Bridget. Of the two she was the more taken by surprise, and immediately Bridget became aware of this, as she did of the fact that the dogs were no strangers to this place.

Mrs Crofton rose to her feet. Her face was pale but her eyes, which had strained wide at the sight of Bridget, were now lowered as she brushed the dry bracken from her skirt, and with her lids still downcast she spoke: 'I'm surprised to see you here.'

'Why?' Although the question was put bluntly and with no hint of the trembling that was threatening to take hold of her limbs, Bridget was fearful of this encounter. At this moment her pity for Mrs Crofton was not to the fore, but neither was any strengthening facet of her character. The traits of Grandma Gether appeared dormant, if not non-existent, and she felt gauche and awkward before this sophisticated woman.

'You don't usually take the dogs out.'

They were staring at each other. The dogs too had become still, lying on their bellies, tongues lolling, following, Bridget knew, a routine. This fact brought a boldness to her retort: 'No, I don't. Laurence usually does when he's at home . . . But of course you are aware of that.'

Mrs Crofton's gaze did not flinch or flicker from Bridget's face, but it was some seconds before she said, 'Yes, I'm aware of it. I often walk over the fells.'

'And through the copse.' Bridget lifted her hand to the surrounding trees. 'It's very out of the way.'

'Why should it be more out of the way for me than for you? We are exactly two and three-quarter miles from my home and just a little more from yours.'

'Practically halfway.'

'What do you mean?'

Yes, what did she mean? In another moment if she wasn't careful, she'd be accusing this woman – but of what? Of being unable to forget a dead love? And it *was* dead. Laurence had said so. 'There's no-one in my life now but you.' She had to believe that. She did believe it. There was no reason why Mrs Crofton shouldn't be resting in this copse during a walk. The fact that she had thought it was Laurence with the dogs proved she didn't know anything concerning his plans and the fact that he was by this time in Holland.

'I said, what do you mean by that?'

'Nothing.'

Again there was silence between them while they stared at each other.

'You are very young, aren't you?'

'Is that a crime?'

'It can be a handicap, a serious handicap.'

'I understood it was an advantage . . . In most cases.'

'It is only an advantage when you want to attract, but it is less than useless when you want to hold anyone . . . a man, a passionate, mature man.'

The blood rushed into Bridget's face. She stood, a child now and vulnerable before this embittered woman, unable to stand up to her, to make any retort on her own behalf.

Now Mrs Crofton's tone altered: her voice dropped and she threw her words like a chain of icicles into Bridget's burning face: 'You'll never hold Laurence, never, neither mentally nor physically. You'll be a plaything for a time . . . a very short time at that. I could be sorry for you if it weren't that you've asked for all that's coming to you, for you've chased him for years, pestered him

with your schoolgirl's pash, and that's what it is
. . . a pash, and he'll treat it like that. And it serves
you right . . . Do you hear? It serves you right.'

Bridget moved slowly back from the white, yet
enraged countenance. Her hands were gripping
the front of her cardigan, and under it, like a
piston running wild, her heart raced. She could
give no answer whatever to this beautiful, tor-
mented creature. She could only deny loudly in
her head all she had said.

'If you go through with it the twenty-ninth
will be one day you'll remember and regret until
you die.'

'Gip . . . Gip, Roy.' As if shouting the dogs'
names would blot out Mrs Crofton's voice,
Bridget called them to her and when they were
running around her feet she cried, 'Come!
Come!' Then swinging about she darted away,
away from the woman who she felt would, even
at this late moment, tear her happiness away
from her. And she ran the few yards to the end
of the copse and over the Dickensons' land as if
Mrs Crofton were at her heels.

When at last she came to a gasping halt she
leant against a boulder and pressed her hands
across her straining ribs. There was only one com-
forting thought in her mind: Mrs Crofton was a
woman without hope. Only a desperately jealous

woman who could see no light ahead would have acted as she had done.

After a moment or so she set off again, with the dogs trotting quietly by her side now. When she reached Balderstone she did not enter the house but after letting the dogs in the front door she turned about and went down the garden towards the pool. She wanted to be by herself for a while longer: if she went indoors she would likely run into someone and be forced to talk, and no doubt have to give some sort of explanation for her strained appearance. But a few minutes by the pool would help her to regain enough composure to carry her through dinner.

A few minutes later Bridget lowered herself onto the grass above the pool. The turbulent surface of the water was churning the pink hue of the sky into lustrous jewels. The glow of the sunset was touching Mickle Fell with gentle fingers, streaking softness down her sides. The carpet of treetops that roofed the forest, on whose outskirts she had recently walked, appeared still now. It was like the stillness inside her, a waiting stillness, for soon the trees would be swaying under the wind that was beginning to drive up the valley, and soon, too, her mind would give way under the pressure of probing. As soon as she was alone for the night it would sink under the hail of questions prompted by Mrs Crofton's bitter words.

Mrs Crofton had said she was young, immature, and she was right. She had longed of late to appear older, to act older, but she really didn't know how to set about it, except by applying heavier make-up. She had never talked brashly, never tried to be witty and bright, except when she displayed some mimicry, but with regard to this she knew that Laurence and her uncle and aunt saw it as the efforts of a young girl . . . and not of an entertaining young woman.

There was a depth of sadness in her eyes as she stared down the valley. There would be rain before morning, and as the days sped into autumn more wind and more rain. Then wind and rain and sleet, and finally snow, until all the valleys and fells would be stilled. The birds would walk on the snow without making footprints. The sheep, those that weren't buried deeply in the white blanket, would huddle on the leeside of the stone walls . . . The winter would be long and hard; they were always long and hard up here. Even as a child she had thought it strange that there was sunshine in other parts of the country while here, and through the Cheviots into Scotland, the sky would be leaden and low, straining as it were to meet with that part of itself it had dropped to the earth.

But then would come the spring. Always after the winter came the spring. It was so simple. If you waited, spring came. If you waited . . . happiness came. The two seemed synonymous with waiting. What would she be feeling like in this coming spring? In the spring she would have been married for six months, have known Laurence intimately for six months.

'Ooh.' The shudder and start she gave were not caused by the thought that had been in her mind but by a figure high up on the rock about the waterfall that fed the pond. Scrambling to her feet she gazed upwards, then in relief said, 'Oh, it's you, Bruce. You did frighten me.'

Bruce Dickenson was of medium height, thickly built, with sandy hair and dark eyes. Bridget had never seen his expression other than kindly. His face was plain, yet overall there was a virile attractiveness about him. But as he dropped down the face of the rock and came towards her now with over cautious steps, Bridget exclaimed to herself in surprise, Good lord! Bruce is tipsy.

And Bruce *was* tipsy. He stood before her smiling. It was a silly self-conscious smile and his voice did not hold his usual brisk north-country accent as he said, 'Hello, Bridget.' It sounded thick and fuddled.

'Hello, Bruce. You startled me.'

'Takin' a short cut . . . often come this way. His nibs would have fits, wouldn't he, if he knew?' He giggled now and Bridget was forced to laugh with him, and she nodded at him, saying, 'He would that.'

'Cuts off . . . cuts off a mile and a half or more when I haven't the van. Bridget.' He swayed gently towards her.

'Yes, Bruce?'

'I'm tight.'

'You can say that again.' She nodded solemnly at him. 'Have you been celebrating?'

'Been to a weddin'. You know Ned Taylor?'

She shook her head.

'Farmer, yon side of Newbiggin. Married a nice girl from Birtley. Grand do.'

'Oh!' It was all Bridget could find to say. She did not know how to deal with . . . this different Bruce.

'May I sit down?'

'Yes, of course, Bruce.'

Slowly the young man lowered himself onto the grass, and leaning back supported himself with his elbows; then looking up at Bridget, he said, 'You sit down an' all. Come on, sit down.'

Bridget sat down, but she did not look at Bruce, nor he at her now. He had fixed his misted gaze on the top of Mickle Fell and he kept it there for some time before saying, 'This bring anything back to you, Bridget?'

'Yes.' She was gazing ahead too. 'Yes, the first time you came up over the cliff wall.' She pointed to where the water was spilling over the edge.

'An' I nearly scared the daylights out of you, although it was moonlight.' He laughed, a thick laugh. 'I'd climbed up there night after night for years just to get the view from this point in the moonlight, and that night . . . there you were.' He turned his head slowly now and leaned it to one side as if it were too heavy to support. 'Won'erful summer that, Bridget. You were seventeen and like a being from the planets. An unawakened princess. Oh, aye.' His head wagged now. 'That's how I used to think of you. Yet they wouldn't have believed it, them over there.' He thumbed over his shoulder. 'They would have killed me if they had found out. Laurence would. Oh aye, he above all of them would have thought it his duty to do me in. And yet I never even kissed you, did I, Bridget? Did I now? Did I?'

Bridget was feeling an uneasy tremor in her stomach; she did not know how to deal with Bruce in his present condition. But it was true what he said. Night after night she had slipped from the house to the pool and they had sat perilously near death on the top of the rock here. One hasty movement and they would have been hurled into the valley below. Sitting dangerously indeed, as Bruce had said. And there were two occasions when Bruce led her down the rock face to the woods below, and he had done nothing but hold her hand: as he had said, he had never kissed her. Now, for the first time, she was realising just what that meant, what control this young man, this virile young man had exercised. The trembling in her stomach eased and she smiled towards him and said quietly, 'You were wonderful to me that summer, Bruce. It was an awful holiday; lonely, that's why I used to come to the pool, but from the time we went adventuring together it was different.'

Bruce's face was straight now, even surly, and he repeated, as if she had not spoken, 'I never kissed you. You were seventeen, a young seventeen, so I never kissed you, but now you're twenty-two and going to be married. Whenever I think of that summer I know I must have been daft, barmy, not to have kissed you.'

The trembling suddenly started again and was stronger now.

'Bridget.' He swung his thick body round until he was kneeling before her, supporting himself again with his hands, but to the front of him now, which made him look like a shaggy pony. But his voice held something of his ordinary tone as he said quickly, 'I've been up here every night for weeks – do you know that, Bridget? – hoping I'd see you. And I'd given up. And now here we are and I'm tight. It isn't as I wanted it ... Bridget,' – he moved forward on his hands – 'you can't marry him. I wanted to tell you, you just can't marry him.'

Bridget moved quickly and pulled herself up. She watched him get to his feet. And then he was standing before her, and she said to him, 'I'm not going to listen to you, Bruce.'

'Oh, yes, you are ... you are, Bridget.'

As she made to turn from him his hands shot out and caught her arms. His hold was not rough but she said, 'Let me go. Please, Bruce, you are hurting me.'

'I wouldn't hurt you, Bridget. You know that, an' I'll let you go when I've had me say, what's been rotting in me since I heard about you and him. I got used to the idea that I didn't stand a chance, not with them lot around you and me tied to the farm. And I would have said nothing an' let things bide if it hadn't been him. But when I knew it was to be him, that dirty swine, I was boiled up.'

'Stop it, Bruce, I won't listen.'

'You don't want to know the truth about him, do you, Bridget? Because if you did you would run a mile afore you'd let him lay a hand on you. He's like his old man, not a pin to choose atween 'em. The old un's running one in Durham now. But I'll say this for him, his woman is without a man, but not so Master Laurence.'

'Leave go, Bruce.'

'No, Bridget, I'll not leave go.' His grip had tightened and his face had become flushed with anger. 'He's got to take a woman with two bairns and the man a decent sort. I know Crofton, I've had business with him. He's a gentleman as neither of your Overmeers will ever be, and our great Master Laurence is his wife's lover.'

'Leave me alone, Bruce, leave me alone, let me go, I'll scream! I don't believe you ... I'll scream!'

'Scream, Bridget, scream. Bring them all here, and then I'll tell him to his face. And you know what I'd say to him? You know what I'd say to him?'

'Let me go!' Bridget was struggling wildly now and her voice was high and breaking into tears.

'You know what I'd say? "Was it cold in Marlow's Hollow last night, Mr Laurence Overmeer?" I'd say, "An' don't you think it's cruel to tie two dogs to a post for hours and bid 'em stay and be quiet?" That's what I'd say.'

'You're lying, you're lying, it's not true. Let me go!'

He released his hold on her arms, and the next moment she was pressed close to him, his whisky-laden breath wafting over her face as he went on thickly but more quietly now, 'It's true, Bridget. He and she were in that hollow for God knows how long. It's just beyond the border of our land on the other side of the wood, as you know. It was the soft whining of the dogs that first drew me notice. I had the ferrets out after rabbits an' I was sitting behind the shrub when I heard 'em, and I stayed to hear more. Aye, Bridget.' He shook her in his hold. 'Aye, I stayed to hear more so that I could convince you.'

She was struggling fiercely, pounding at his chest, kicking at his shins, 'Let me go! I'll scream, I'll scream, and they'll come.'

'Let them come . . . that's what I want. Let them come.' His voice had risen now almost to a shout. 'Let them find us together; he hasn't a leg to stand on. I could have had you, Bridget, if I hadn't been such a fool. I know now that if I'd played me cards right you would have come away with me. My father says it would have been all right with him. I told him about it. Bridget, it's not too late . . . and you can stop struggling, you can't get away.'

All of a sudden Bridget stopped struggling. She became limp in his hold and, looking into his face, pleaded, 'Bruce, please, please let me go . . . there'll only be trouble.'

'Do you believe what I said, Bridget?'

'Let me go, Bruce, please. I beseech you, let me go.'

'Do you believe what I said, Bridget?'

She shook her head wildly.

'He's a swine. The minute you're married, he'll go on the same as his father did, don't you understand? Last night those two were at each other like love-starved savages.'

'Stop it! Stop it!' Her voice was really a scream now, and on this she felt herself lifted from her feet and carried forward. When she realised he was taking her into the hut she struggled and cried, 'No, Bruce! No!' and for a moment she stopped their progress by gripping the stanchion of the door. But then with a jerk they were rocketed inside and into comparative darkness. Her body had become rigid and her mind so frozen that she could make no protesting sound when he said, 'I love you, Bridget. It's not too late. I've got to make you listen to me. Kiss me, Bridget. Kiss me.'

It must have been her startling spasm of energy, together with the cracket – a three-legged stool which she sometimes used when she was painting – which caused Bruce to topple her over backwards. As she felt herself being brought to the ground with him a scream escaped her, and for a moment blackness engulfed her as a searing pain shot through her neck and shoulders.

'You hurt, Bridget? Oh, my God. Have I hurt you? Bridget, speak to me.'

She opened her eyes and looked into his face, twisted now with genuine concern, and she murmured tremulously, 'Oh, Bruce.'

In his fuddled state Bruce must have taken her tone and quiet attitude for acceptance to his pleas, for the next moment her head and shoulders were lifted from the floor and his arms were around her, and so great was the pain now in her shoulder that his kisses brought no protest from her for some moments. And then she could only protest weakly with one hand as she gasped, 'No, Bruce! No, Bruce!'

It was at the point when he seemed to be snatched away from her that the blackness of deep night descended on her . . .

When she regained consciousness it was to imagine that she was clawing her way up the face of the cliff in inky blackness, and she gasped for air as she flung an arm upwards to get a grip on the slippery surface. When her fingers felt a hard substance beneath them they dug themselves in and she hung on, until she tried to raise her other arm, and then she was shot blindingly into awareness, and for a moment she imagined she was dead and travelling the strange road of the dead, or that she had suddenly gone mad, for she was being carried on some weird vehicle that jolted her body, and each movement rent her with excruciating pain. She imagined the strange vehicle was carrying her up the rowan walk. She closed her eyes tightly and tried to remember what had happened. When, with thankful suddenness, the pain eased she saw herself floating away from the strange contraption on which she had been lying, then her uncle's voice checked her as it called loudly, 'Bridget! Bridget!' Now another voice, which she recognised as Ned Ryder's, was saying, 'I couldn't leave her there, couldn't chance it, sir. I knocked him out with the butt of me gun.'

She felt arms beneath her, her uncle's arms, and they brought the pain to the fore again, causing it to spurt its protest from her mouth in a loud yell. Following this there was complete nothingness.

When Bridget finally regained consciousness she remembered with a chilling clarity most of what had happened, and she lay with her eyes closed repeating to herself, 'Oh, dear Lord. Oh, dear Lord.' She had a strong feeling that she should pray, but for what? And for whom? For herself, for Laurence, for Bruce? The name of Bruce coming into her mind brought no condemnation with it. She could feel sad for Bruce, and he had told her the truth. She tried to shut her mind against the memory of his words but the door was wide open and could never again be closed. She felt in some strange way that the years of her life that had gone before, twenty-two full years, were as nothing, as if they were the time she had spent in her mother's womb and only now was she drawing her first breath. Never again would she be surrounded by mists of fantasy; no more would her dreamy character be a screen behind which she could hide and peep out at the world . . . at people she liked, and withdraw when confronted by people she didn't like.

Her aunt's voice came to her, whispering, 'It can't be true. Are you sure, Ryder?'

'Yes, ma'am, as sure as I have eyes. I had to pull him away. I was up near the greenhouses and on my way to the cottage to get me gun when I thought I heard her calling. I took no notice at first, thinking I was mistaken, then something made me go down. I always thought that was a dangerous place. You could slip over the side—'

'Yes, yes, Ryder, but go on.'

'Well, ma'am, as I told the master, I'm no match for Bruce Dickenson with me hands but, as I said, I had me gun with me. I was going down to the north boundary after them rabbits. They've started there again, ma'am.'

'Yes, yes.' Sarah Overmeer closed her eyes for a moment. 'You say you knocked him unconscious, that his head was bleeding badly. How is it then that he's not there, now?'

'He's a tough customer, is young Dickenson, ma'am. I know that I knocked him completely out because he was limp as a sack when I pulled him aside, but he must have recovered and scutted . . . I mean, made his way home. I was frightened to leave her there and the garden truck was just at the bottom of the walk, so I put her on it. I thought it was the best way.'

'You did very well, Ryder. Very well indeed under the circumstances. Thank you. But remember what the master told you: this must be kept quiet.'

'Yes, ma'am.'

'Go out now and see if there's any sign of Mr John. He hasn't taken the car, so he must be walking. MacKay's gone the village way. You take the fell road.'

'Yes, ma'am, right away.'

There was a sound of a door closing, then Bridget was conscious of her aunt standing over her, and she heard her murmur, almost in anguish, 'My God!'

There came a lull in Bridget's thinking. It seemed that she slept, yet she was aware of movement about her, but it wasn't until she heard John's voice that she opened her eyes and knew herself to be lying on the broad couch in the drawing-room. John had his back to her and was talking to some figures out of her sight. One of them said, 'Do you mean to suggest Ryder is deliberately lying?' This was Vance Overmeer speaking.

'Yes, if he says that he saw Bruce Dickenson attacking her.'

'Well, I know which of the two I'd believe if it came to the push.'

'So do I.'

'John.' Sarah Overmeer's voice turned the name into a command. 'You must examine her.'

'What!'

'You're a doctor, aren't you? Why shouldn't you?'

'For the simple reason that I'm not going to. I've put her shoulder right and that was put out by a fall—'

'When Bruce Dickenson threw her to the ground . . . And how do you know if there's nothing further wrong unless you examine her?'

'I tell you I know there isn't. Anyway there'll be plenty of time to find out by asking her when she comes round, won't there?'

'You're just trying to be difficult, John, aren't you? All right! All right! Go on defending a drunken sot. Time alone will prove who's right.'

When Bridget saw her aunt's figure coming hastily towards her she closed her eyes and feigned sleep. She must have time to think. Time to get on top of the pain: not the pain in her shoulder but the pain in her mind, for unless she could to some extent control this pain it would destroy her. In an odd way she felt at war with the pain in her mind. If it won she would, she knew, be a weakling for the rest of her life, putting up with humiliation and shame rather than facing the truth, the truth that Bruce had brought out of the shadows.

Three

'Listen to me, Bridget, you must tell me all that happened. Don't you realise, child, the importance of remembering what happened?' Sarah's voice rose on the last words, and she leant forward from her chair, drawn close to the bedside, towards Bridget.

Bridget closed her eyes for a moment and through her lids felt the mellow light and warmth of the sun streaming through the window onto the bed. For the last hour the sun had played full on her but she felt its effect only on her skin. Inside, her body was numb with a cold dead numbness that suggested it would never thaw.

'Bridget!'

At the sharp command she opened her eyes, and looking straight at her aunt, said, 'I've told you all that happened.'

'Ryder said—'

Bridget suddenly put her good hand up to her ear and shook her head violently as she cried, 'I don't want to hear what Ryder said, Aunt Sarah. Please! Please! Anyway, Bruce was drunk. I've told you he kissed me and that was all.'

'How you can lie there and defend him, I don't know. You'd better not defend him in front of your uncle. If your uncle finds him . . .'

Bridget's head became still and she asked flatly, 'Why is uncle trying to find him when you want to hush the matter up?'

Sarah Overmeer found herself in the unusual position of being at a disadvantage. Her lids drooped, then stretched wide. 'We only want to hush it up, as you term it, for your sake, my dear. It's not the kind of thing one wants whispered around the county a few days before your wedding, is it? Even if, as you say, he only kissed you.'

'There won't be any wedding.'

Bridget was looking over her aunt's shoulder towards the wide expanse of sky from where the warmth was pouring, and then the bright light was blotted from her face as Sarah Overmeer sprang to her feet and whispered angrily, 'What are you saying? Then something did happen? Look, Bridget, I don't want to get angry with you when you're in this state but . . .'

Bridget laid her head back against the pink satin-padded headrest, and looking wearily at her aunt, said, 'Yes, something did happen, but not what you think.'

Sarah Overmeer drew in a deep breath, then exhaled slowly, before saying quietly and in a restrained tone, 'Then may I ask what made you say such a silly thing? Come along now, tell me.'

Bridget was staring up into the austere face and she now drew in a long breath which she too let out before saying, 'I've changed my mind.'

'You have *what*!'

Bridget made no reply, and Sarah, jerking the chair towards the bed again and seating herself close to Bridget, hissed in a voice streaked with anger, 'Changed your mind? This business has unbalanced you. There was no such thought as changing your mind when you saw Laurence off yesterday, was there?'

'No, Aunt Sarah.'

Something in Bridget's tone caused Sarah Overmeer to draw in her chin and bring her lids down to peer at Bridget as if trying to get her into focus. 'Then' – her voice and manner softened again – 'can't you see, my dear, it's this dreadful business of last night that has upset you? But it's only momentarily; it will pass. John says you have received a shock, but in a day or so you'll be yourself again. And . . . and remember what I told you in our little talk the other evening . . . once you are married.'

Their eyes held, neither knowing at this moment what exactly was in the other's mind. Then Bridget said, 'I feel tired, Aunt Sarah.'

There followed a short silence. Sarah Overmeer was not used to being dismissed, but whatever she was feeling, her manner now showed only concern.

'Yes, yes, my dear, you're bound to feel tired; your poor shoulder. Just you rest quietly; that's what you need, rest. Of course, you're tired. Now I'll away and let you sleep.'

The fact that her Aunt Sarah was repeating herself was evidence that she was very disturbed. Bridget watched her leave the room, then closed her eyes. She did feel tired, and not only tired but different: older, and a woman. It was, she thought, as if she had lived many lives and was tired of them all. She was tired in body and mind. Her body felt bruised and beaten, but she wasn't concerned by the state of her body; it was the change in her mind that was startling her. All night long she had thought, and fought, and this morning she knew, but without any sense of triumph, that she had won.

She looked back to herself standing on the platform in Durham station returning Laurence's blown kiss. That had been her . . . she had been Bridget Gether then, not Bridget Gether now. Never again would she be that Bridget Gether.

That particular Bridget had known that Joyce Crofton had been Laurence's mistress but she had believed Laurence when he said, 'There's no-one now but you.' But this Bridget, this Bridget that had been born overnight, knew that the past tense didn't apply to Laurence's association with Mrs Crofton . . . What were the words that Bruce had used? They were at each other like love-starved savages.

A few days before his marriage he was loving Mrs Crofton like a savage, and after their marriage he would go on loving her like a savage, and at the same time he would expect her herself to love him, and he would become angry, even mad when she didn't. She had already had a taste of his displeasure in this way.

She knew now that during the past six months he had been comparing her with Mrs Crofton. She recalled an incident, forgotten until this moment. He had taken her to see a film in Newcastle. It was the love story of a woman, a voluptuous woman, who had been married three times, but still could not forget the love of her youth, and when years later they met again nothing was spared in depicting their reunion. The picture seemed to have impressed Laurence. He was quiet as they drove back to Balderstone, but of a sudden, apropos of nothing that had gone before, at least since they had entered the car, he said, 'Did you like it?' She knew instantly what he meant and she answered, 'In parts.' Then he had repeated, 'In parts?' and some minutes later he had spoken almost to himself as he said, 'She could love, that one, she was ravenous for love.'

Bridget knew now that all the time Laurence had been watching that film he had been seeing himself and Mrs Crofton.

Then why? Why, if he loved her like that and she him, had she not made a break with her husband? Divorce was an ordinary everyday occurrence now. It didn't matter in what stratum of society you were, it was accepted. Then why? Why? Bruce had said that Mr Crofton was a nice man.

The name Bruce stopped her thinking at this point, and she looked as an outsider might into her own mind and was more than surprised to find that it was thinking of Bruce Dickenson without bitterness, even with tenderness. Perhaps it was as he had said, if he had made love to her on those romantic nights instead of playing the gallant squire, who knows but some spark might have set off her love at a tangent away from the one person who had always filled her mind and girlish dreams.

For eighteen years she had been conscious more or less of Laurence, of the attraction he had for her. This being so, was it possible that this feeling could be eliminated in a few hours? In a few minutes? But it hadn't been eliminated . . . part of it remained. The fascination of him still held her, but with a difference. It no longer cloaked her in a silver mist. No longer was he standing within the white light of the absolute singleness of her love. She was seeing him for the first time in her life as he really was. A charming, ruthless, utterly selfish, passionate individual. A man who always had his own way and would continue to have it as long as he lived. Whether he would be touched or pained by the trouble this caused was doubtful. She felt a sense of shame that she had always been aware of his true character but had buried the knowledge, willingly buried it.

She remembered being scornful of writers who described love as partly pain, but now she both understood and believed this, for what remained of her love for Laurence was the fascination and the pain.

There was a tap on the bedroom door and her uncle called, 'Bridget!'

When Vance Overmeer stood towering above her she found she couldn't look at him. This man had passed something on to his son. All his life he, too, had gone his own road, causing what depth of suffering to Aunt Sarah; the unimaginable suffering of a strong woman. She felt a moment's alarm when she thought he might touch her – it was as if Laurence himself were standing there. Instead he said, 'How is it feeling?'

Bridget looked down at her strapped arm as she replied, 'The pain has eased.'

'That's good, that's good; it will be all right for the wedding. That's the main thing, isn't it?' He was smiling widely, a false stiff smile, as he bent above her. She knew he was aware of what she had said to Aunt Sarah but it had been arranged that he ignore it.

She could not restrain herself from saying curtly, 'Aunt Sarah must have told you, Uncle Vance, that I have changed my mind.'

She almost felt the tremor that coursed through the long body, and his words seemed to ride on panic as he brought out, 'You can't do this. Whatever nonsense you have got in your head, get rid of it. Your marriage to Laurence will take place on the twenty-ninth. Now understand that, Bridget.'

Her eyes were wide as she stared up at him, and if she wanted the proof of the change in herself she had it in the note of defiance in her reply. 'You cannot make me marry Laurence if I don't wish to, Uncle. I'm of age, you know.' She dared to speak to Uncle Vance like that! She was startled further by the effect her words were having on the man at her side, for he was moving his neck in his impeccable stiff white collar as if it were strangling him, and for a full minute he stumbled on words in a blustering, unintelligible way, before saying, 'I'll . . . I'll kill that Dickenson when I lay hands on him.'

'My decision has nothing to do with Bruce Dickenson, Uncle.'

They considered each other for a while before, on a deep swallow, he said simply, 'No?'

'No. Nothing whatever.'

'Then what is making you take this attitude?'

'I have changed my mind, that's all. We will go into it further when Laurence returns. That's . . . that's if I'm here then.' She glanced at her arm. 'As soon as I'm able, I'm going to Grandma's.'

Vance Overmeer continued to stare at Bridget

for some seconds before abruptly turning from her. Then he almost broke into a run as he made to leave the room.

Kate came up at one o'clock with the lunch tray. Kate was forty-eight, unmarried and romantic, and she worshipped Mr Laurence, whether in spite of, or because of, his way of life no-one but Kate knew. But now, as she arranged the bed table carefully over Bridget's legs, she said, 'You'll soon be all right, Miss Bridget. When Mr Laurence comes home he'll put you right.' She gave a tap to the napkin, then bestowed a wide thoughtless smile on Bridget as she imparted the information: 'He should be home the night, or in the mornin' at the latest.'

The tray almost bounced off the bed and Kate exclaimed, 'Oh, Miss Bridget! Oh, Miss Bridget! Steady.'

'What did you say?'

'There now, you'll have it over again. I was just sayin' that Mr Laurence'll be back the night, so the master says . . . he's flying.'

'Who told you this?'

'Well, miss.' Kate straightened her apron and wagged her head slightly. 'We all know it. I was to clear some of Mr Laurence's things from his room to the one in the west wing – you know, miss, getting the room ready for when you come back from your honeymoon – an' I was actually at the job when the mistress comes up and says to leave things be as Mr Laurence was expected back. It's because of your fall, Miss Bridget.' Kate paused here and gave Bridget a long scrutinising glance.

The look not only penetrated into Bridget but told her that Kate was aware to some extent that the fall had been no ordinary one. You cannot shut mouths; you can forbid them to open, and Aunt Sarah and Uncle Vance had undoubtedly done that, but their power apparently was not omnipotent – there was knowledge in Kate's eyes. She made herself say calmly, 'Thank you, Kate, I can manage.'

'Very well, miss.'

Kate departed, and Bridget, staring down at the silver-covered dishes before her, put her hand on one hot surface without feeling the heat and, pressing it there, said, 'I won't, I can't, I won't see him. What will I say?'

It was the girl of yesterday returned, but it was the woman of today who answered quietly, 'Tell him the truth, that is all you can do.' But this new being was so new that for a moment she doubted its strength. She must talk to John. That's if he would listen. He had been curt with her when he was in a while ago. He seemed pre-occupied, engrossed with his own thoughts. He had asked her nothing about the events of last night, or Bruce, and she herself had not brought up the subject.

She pushed the tray aside and, getting out of bed, struggled into her dressing-gown. It was only a quarter to one: the lunch bell hadn't gone yet, so they had sent her tray up early.

Within a few minutes she was knocking on John's door.

'Yes? Come in.'

He certainly hadn't expected to see her for his eyebrows shot up and he said in surprise, but harshly, 'What are you doing up?'

'I wanted to talk to you.'

'Couldn't it have waited? Have you had your lunch? It's almost one o'clock.'

To these two questions she replied, 'My lunch is waiting for me but I just had to talk to you first . . . They've sent for Laurence.'

'Sent for him?' He moved towards her. 'Who told you that?'

'Kate let it out.'

He stood looking down at her for a moment, before he said, 'Is it because of what happened last night with Bruce? Are you going to make an issue out of it? There's nothing wrong with you,

you know. I've seen Bruce. He might have been tight but he remembers everything. He wouldn't hurt a hair of your head.' He sounded bitter and she said hastily, 'It has nothing to do with Bruce, although Aunt Sarah is making out it has. It's because . . .' She looked away from him. 'Because I told her that I wasn't going to marry Laurence.'

He looked at her for a moment before he asked, 'Why?'

'I have my reasons.'

'Mrs Crofton?'

She brought her eyes up to his, 'Yes.' If she expected commendation for her decision she was disappointed, for turning from her and walking to the window he said, 'It'll be a different tune when you are confronted by him. He'll just hand you some plausible explanation and you'll fall on his neck.'

She felt as if she had been slapped in the face. John, of all people, speaking to her like that. The tears began to smart the back of her eyes, but she was able to stem their flow with the anger that was rising in her.

'We'll see. But it's of no account. I'm sorry to have troubled you with my petty concerns.'

She had reached the door when his arm came across her shoulder and with the flat of his hand he kept the door closed. And his voice was soft and full of regret as he whispered, 'I'm sorry, Bridget; forgive me for I'm all tensed up. You know that all that happens to you is of concern to me. You know that, don't you?'

When she did not answer, he went on, 'Don't cry. Don't cry, Bridget, just stick to your guns. It'll be hard going, I warn you, but in the end you'll be thankful.' His face was close to hers now, his gaze tender and warm as he added, 'You've got to be happy.'

She could scarcely see him through her misted eyes, but her voice held a cynical note when she replied, 'It's an odd time to talk of me being happy, isn't it, when I'm cancelling my wedding.'

'It'll pass like a bad dream.'

'Thank you, Doctor.'

He straightened up, 'Don't be cynical, Bridget. It doesn't suit you, so leave that for the sophisticated dames.'

'You too would like me to remain the little gullible girl, wouldn't you, John?'

'No, no, I wouldn't.' His tone was harsh again. 'You've been that long enough, much too long, but you've got to walk into womanhood; you can't jump the gap.'

'I'm the exception, John.'

He looked hard at her; then moving away

from the door he said quietly, 'Then I hope you've brought courage with you, for you're going to need it.'

The lunch bell rang and Bridget opened the door and went out without further words. Was it because *she* had changed that she imagined that John had changed, too? Perhaps, perhaps.

At about two o'clock Sarah Overmeer came into the bedroom, dressed for town. Her manner was casual, even offhand, and she showed some annoyance at Bridget being out of bed. 'I'm going into Newcastle,' she said. 'I may not be back until this evening. Now you must get back into bed and rest.'

'I would like to go downstairs, Aunt Sarah.'

'Nonsense. You are still suffering from shock. It is much better that you stay where you are.' Sarah bent from her height and straightened the coverlet on the bed.

'I don't feel ill, Aunt Sarah. I would be much better downstairs.'

'You know you can't dress with your arm like that.'

'I can get into some of my things. Kate will help me, and I can wear a dressing-gown.'

Sarah Overmeer pressed her lips together before saying, 'Well, you can stay up for a while;

I'll tell Kate. But you are not to come downstairs. You are being very naughty, you know, Bridget, naughty altogether.'

It was difficult not to make the reply, I'm being natural, Aunt Sarah. What you are finding is that I am no longer pliable; I am no longer utterly biddable.

After a short silence Sarah said briskly, 'Well, I must away. I'll send Kate up to help you. Your uncle should be in shortly; I have left a note for him. Promise me you will just sit quietly.'

'I'll just sit quietly, Aunt Sarah.'

Was there mockery in the reply? It brought a stretching to Sarah's face and she turned abruptly and made for the door, only to stop, turn once again, but slowly now, and after a pause during which she kept her eyes fixed on Bridget, say, 'I'm going to ask you a question, Bridget.'

Again there was a pause, while Bridget waited without murmur. 'Have you in any way encouraged Bruce Dickenson over the past few months?'

'Encouraged?' Bridget's voice faded away on the word, then she brought out almost vehemently, 'What do you mean, Aunt Sarah? I have been engaged to Laurence for the past six months and you are suggesting that I have at the same time been encouraging Bruce . . . ?'

'There is no need to get yourself agitated; we only wondered.'

'Wondered?' Bridget's voice was sharp and high and her aggressive attitude was no doubt causing some perplexity to Sarah Overmeer. This was not the Bridget that she had known and even ruled for years. She said now, 'What has come over you? Why do you use that tone to me?'

'Why do you suggest such a thing to me, Aunt Sarah?'

'I only wanted to find out if there was anything more behind that man's attitude; whether it was an attack or—'

'Or, Aunt Sarah? Or what? Are you suggesting that last night was just another meeting, part of a habit say, one that we couldn't break?' Bridget checked her outburst. In another minute she would have said, I don't happen to be like your son; I have no habits that I'm unable to break. She bowed her head, only to bring it up sharply again as Sarah said, 'We were only trying to be fair to the man.'

'Fair to Bruce Dickenson! Fair to any of the Dickensons . . . Ooh! Aunt Sarah.'

Sarah Overmeer was not only perplexed now but deeply disturbed. She could not understand the change in this girl. If she weren't hearing her with her own ears she would not have believed it. Perhaps it was the result of shock. Pray God it was, anyway. There was going to be great difficulty in persuading or dealing with her in her present state, but she must deal with her, she must persuade her. She must be made to conform, to keep her promise and marry Laurence. That was vital. Where would they all be if this wedding didn't go through? The thought spurred her departure to Newcastle. She said abruptly, 'I will see you as soon as I return, Bridget. Goodbye.'

Vance Overmeer did not come up to see Bridget, and when at half-past four Kate brought up the tea-tray the answer she gave to Bridget's enquiry was that the master had not yet come in.

Bridget was sitting, one arm in her dressing-gown, near the window. She kept her gaze directed towards where two herring gulls were wheeling slowly in circles, still-winged on a current of air. The sun was shining on their breasts and underwings and their slow effortless-ness spoke to her of such harmony that she envied them their existence, even while she forced herself to ask a question of Kate, 'Have you heard when Mr Laurence is expected Kate?'

There was a full and significant pause before Kate replied, and then she spoke hastily and briefly. 'No, miss, I've heard nothin'.'

Kate had learned from the kitchen, and Nancy, that she had made a mistake in carrying the news upstairs. And she had wondered in the thick jumble of her mind why the mistress hadn't gone for her for telling Miss Bridget the news. When it dawned on her that Miss Bridget hadn't given her away, in fact, had said nothing whatever about it to the mistress, she was more puzzled than ever. There was something here that was funny and she'd better keep her mouth shut or there would be trouble for her.

After Kate had left the room Bridget continued to look at the gulls. They spoke to her of freedom, and, of a sudden her whole being was longing for freedom: to be away, away from this house that had been home to her, or partly so; but more so, away from the people in it, those whose outer lives she saw quite clearly now were a façade. Everyone was pretending, everyone, in a way, was dishonest. Her Uncle Vance, her Aunt Sarah, and Laurence. Yes, Laurence most of all. The form of dishonesty was in the servants too: in Kate, and in Ryder. But perhaps she was being over-harsh, at least on the latter two . . . they had their orders, they were earning their living, and Ryder particularly would class his attitude as loyalty. Then there was John. But John did not belong to Balderstone, at least not any more. Yet wasn't he too acting? Why had he suddenly taken to going out so much when he wasn't really fit? It looked as if he were being compelled . . . to take walks. Last night, this morning, and now this afternoon. She wouldn't have known about this latest walk if, half an hour before, she hadn't chanced to look down onto the drive and seen him leaving not by the main door but appearing on the drive by way of the courtyard, which meant he had used the back staircase again.

John's duplicity aroused in her a peculiar kind of pain and she rose to her feet, saying to herself, I've got to get away. I'll to to Grandma's; I'll go tomorrow. I'll wire tonight. She'll send Frances to London to meet me.

From half-past five, when Kate had returned to take away the tea-tray, Bridget had seen no-one, nor had she heard any sound in the house; it was as if the whole place was deserted except for herself.

It was usual for the first bell to ring at seven o'clock to give warning of approaching dinner. This was a custom that Sarah Overmeer had installed, and badgered the family into keeping rigidly over the years of her marriage. The custom laid claim to a tradition that was almost, except in exclusive houses, no longer in practice. And it had never been in practice in the days when her stepmother ruled the house. Hester Gether would have laughed to scorn such ceremonial pomp. But such ritual formed the iron bands around the casing of Sarah Overmeer's life.

Yet it was seven o'clock and no bell had rung. That meant that neither her Aunt Sarah nor her Uncle Vance had returned home yet. Perhaps they had both gone to meet Laurence to give him the details before he entered the house; and when they returned, what then? She could see him now filling the doorway. The picture brought her to her feet. She couldn't bear the thought of him coming into her room. If she saw him here she would also see Mrs Crofton, as plainly as if she were in the flesh. The idea was nauseating. Wherever she was to meet him, it couldn't be here. She must go downstairs. Like this? She looked down at the sweeping drift of quilted dove-grey satin that went to make up the dressing-gown she was wearing. Aunt Sarah didn't like people parading about the house in a dressing-gown. Moreover, she had said she wasn't to go downstairs.

She moved firmly towards the door. Surprisingly, Aunt Sarah's likes and dislikes had ceased to intimidate her. She would settle herself in the drawing-room and there they would find her when they returned.

At the head of the staircase she gripped the rail with her good hand to steady her descent. Her legs felt unbelievably weak and the feeling annoyed her. But she told herself it wouldn't do to trip in the folds of the dressing-gown. Her mind went off at a tangent and she thought, I must cut some off the bottom, even if it spoils the line, for it's much too long. I should never have bought it in the first place. And then she thought, It's a shame to cut it, I'll send it to Yvonne. By the time she reached the bottom of the stairs she almost said aloud, What does it matter? Why are you bothering to think about a paltry dressing-gown?

The hall was deserted. The front door was closed, there was even no sound coming from the direction of the kitchen. Where was everyone? She went into the drawing-room, where the huge electric imitation log fire was alight. Instead of sitting on the couch that stood in front of it, she drew an armchair close up to the fire, for she found she was shivering. She did not question whether it was with cold, or with apprehension, she only knew that she was aware of every muscle in her body vibrating.

After some moments she asked herself if she should ring for Kate and ask what time dinner was to be served. But no, she would wait. Someone would come soon.

At about half-past seven she heard footsteps making for the dining-room. They were those of MacKay, but he did not enter the drawing-room. Apparently there was no need, as everything was ready for his mistress's return, the room warm and one of the French windows ajar. Sarah Overmeer could not bear stuffiness.

The clock showed a quarter to eight when Bridget heard the front door open, and she knew immediately that Laurence had returned, together with his parents. In a moment one or other was almost sure to enter this room, and now the thought of facing any of them, Laurence in particular, seemed out of the question. She wasn't up to it. Why had she thought it would be easier to let them find her here?

She rose to her feet and moved hastily towards the French windows. Pushing them further open, she stood within the framework.

To stand like this with her back to them would give her, she imagined, some little advantage. They would exclaim upon her presence downstairs and then she would turn slowly and walk forward. She was rehearsing her movements frantically in her mind as if she were about to make a first-night entry onto a stage, when from the distance she heard muffled footsteps crossing the hall. She heard her aunt's voice and someone answering. Whether it was her uncle or Laurence she couldn't make out. Her body was stiff, her strapped shoulder was aching, and she felt slightly sick. When she heard footsteps outside the drawing-room door her breath checked itself to a stop as she waited, but the door did not open. Instead, along the balcony in front of her there flashed into the twilight a streak of light. They had gone into the study. It was like a reprieve and her chest sank as if her body had been suddenly deflated.

Were they all in the study? She had her answer almost immediately as her uncle's voice came to her clearly, saying, 'I want to get one point straight before your mother comes in. Did you or did you not see the Crofton woman after she left here the other evening?'

'Don't call her the Crofton woman or I might retaliate and say, "Have you seen that slut in Durham lately?"'

Laurence's words had hit the air like bullets

from a gun, and as effectively they seemed to have silenced his father. But apparently it was only rage that had checked Vance Overmeer's reply, for now there came to Bridget a spate of words that made her bow her head and press herself back against the stanchion of the door as if to evade their impact. It was hard for her to believe that the two men within feet of her were father and son, for they were exchanging words like men of the same age, the same passions, but without any blood tie. They were like combatants. Vance Overmeer's voice had sunk almost to a steely whisper and his tone was unlike any that Bridget had heard before, for always he sounded docile when he spoke to his wife. 'However I run my life and whoever is in it is my affair. The only one who has any right to question me is your mother. And let me tell you this: for quite a time before and after I married her I kept up some semblance of decency. I certainly didn't seek entertainment shortly before my wedding.'

'Don't put it like that!' The words were spaced and grim, and Bridget found she was clutching her throat tightly with her hand. 'Anyway, what are you getting at? What makes you think—?'

'Were you with her? That's what I'm asking you.'

There came a pause, during which Bridget

found herself straining her ears for the reply, and when it came she closed her eyes. 'No, of course I wasn't. What do you take me for?' The words rang so true that Bridget felt a surge of relief rushing through her, but the relief was momentary, for she recalled Bruce Dickenson's voice describing what he had seen, and strangely she knew that if put to the test, even before this, she would have believed Bruce Dickenson before the man who was to have been her husband. And then the truth of Bruce's words were confirmed in the next few minutes, for she heard her Uncle Vance, in harsh grating tones, say, 'Look, Laurence, it's important you come clean now, at least to me. Bridget's got hold of something, and apparently it has nothing to do with what happened between her and young Dickenson, but Henry Dickenson, when I saw him last night and threatened what I was going to do, answered me too calmly for good, for he said, "Do that. Just do that. Shoot him on sight, as you say you're going to, and then the matter will come into the open, into court, and my son . . . if he's alive . . . will be able to tell a jury why he went to see Miss Bridget; the reason being an incident that took place in Marlow's Hollow last night between your son and a certain lady. If he's not alive then, I'll do the telling." That's what he said. Now what have you got to say?'

The silence was long and painful. It seemed to come as a tangible wave from out of the study and cover the balcony and overflow into the darkening night, until it was pierced by Vance Overmeer's harsh whisper, 'You blasted fool!'

'All right, all right, you needn't rub it in. It was for the last time; it couldn't be helped.'

'There'll never be a last time between you and her, and you know it. Why the devil didn't you take her away years ago? It would have solved your problems.'

'I've told you before.' Laurence's voice came flat now, dead sounding. 'They're Catholics; he won't divorce her. And besides, she's fond of the children.'

'My God! Still that? Well, all I can say is you're going to have your work cut out to undo that last piece of indulgence. Bridget knows something, I'm positive of that. That swine Dickenson likely told her.'

'In that case, it's all up a gum tree, isn't it?' Laurence's voice, sounding almost indifferent, cut through Bridget like a knife. Closing her lids tightly, she tried to check the flow of tears raining down her face.

'Don't be ridiculous!' Vance Overmeer's voice

came strong again from the study. 'The wedding must take place, you know that as well as I do. It must take place; we're sunk otherwise, completely sunk. She holds more than half the shares in Baxter's, and without them Vandermeer won't look at our proposal ... What did he say?'

'Well, there wasn't much time to get down to anything before I got your message, but I get the impression that if we could put up fifty thousand for a start he'd bite.'

'Fifty thousand? My God! Fifty thousand! Fifty thousand and we'd be on our feet firmly, and with the new factory underway.'

'I was never for the other factory, you know that. It was too much a drain on our capital. And look what it has done. I was right.'

'You are right only if we don't have Bridget's money behind us. If you hadn't been such a blasted fool, in another few days everything would have been as safe as the Bank of England.'

'Well, I have been a blasted fool, so drop it, for God's sake ... and suppose we don't get the use of her money, just suppose. Would it be any use trying the bank again?'

'No, I tapped Burnett after I'd seen you off, just in case. He indicated straight away that I could save my breath. Our red is red to the tune of seventy-five thousand. We are as near as dammit bankrupt . . . Look, Laurence, we are right up against it. If we sink, the lot goes . . . everything. You don't quite take in what that means, you've had it so easy so long. Look here, Laurence, you go to Bridget, make a clean breast of it, throw yourself on her mercy. There's nothing satisfies a woman so much as being able to forgive. I wish I had learned that earlier on. My life would have been smoother and easier. Once you are married you can go your own road again: only do it cautiously, have sense.'

Bridget had the sensation of choking. The breath was being pressed out of her by a mixture of emotions: incredible astonishment, shame, a feeling of being degraded and, threading them all, a cord of anger. She felt she could not bear to hear another word. If she heard one thing more her heart would burst. She was pulling herself away from the support of the door when she heard her Aunt Sarah's voice breaking in on that of the men, saying firmly, 'Well, what have you decided?' So she was forced to remain to hear the answer.

'Nothing much, except that the marriage must go through. By hook or by crook it must go through.'

'For once I agree with you, Vance.' The voice

was cool, as cool as the night air had suddenly become. 'And it's just as well the wedding day is so near, for you may well have to shoulder an unexpected responsibility.'

'What do you mean?' Laurence's words were slow and thick sounding and brought Bridget right onto the balcony now, her eyes staring towards the study windows.

'I mean there may be results of Bruce Dickenson's attack last night. I can't think of anything else at the moment that would make her want to put off the wedding. I also think she has got a sneaking regard for the fellow.'

'You're saying . . . You mean there might be . . . ?'

'Just that.'

'Well, my God! I didn't bargain for this.'

'There were lots of things you didn't bargain for, Laurence. If there is an outcome it must have your name.'

'Very nice, very nice. And what about Dickenson?'

'What about him? It is unlikely that he'll remember much. He was drunk and then he had his head split open by Ryder, as I've told you already.'

'What if Ryder talks?'

'He won't.'

'What if the Dickensons talk?'

'I don't think you need worry about them, they are not blabbers, whatever else they are. And it wouldn't be to the young one's benefit to admit he was trespassing and attacked a young girl. This Ryder would bear out if necessary . . . Now before we do anything more let us eat. Dinner is ready. Go in. I'll join you in a moment, but first I must go upstairs and prepare her for your visit. And you must act quite naturally, Laurence. You have come home because you heard of her being attacked.' Sarah Overmeer stopped talking for a moment, then said, 'Oh, come in, Kate.'

Bridget could no longer see the light, for her face was awash with tears and her body was suffering under the pressure of all the sorrow in the world, deep shame-filled sorrow. Sorrow for the three people in the room there, people whom she had known all her life and in different ways had loved and respected. They were county folk, looked up to on all sides, but they were no better than a band of crooks. Kate's voice came to her now, saying excitedly, 'She's not in her room, ma'am, Miss Bridget's not in her room. I can't see her nowhere . . . anywhere.'

'Have you looked in the drawing-room?'

'Yes, ma'am, all over, and—'

Kate's voice was shut off from Bridget now by the terrifying sounds of her own crying. It blotted out the sudden commotion in the study. The sound coming from her wide-open mouth mounted into a whirl: she could hear nothing but the awful sound of her own anguish and could see only dimly the figures on the terrace, the faces all ran into one with an expression of horrified amazement. She was mouthing words now, yelling them at the top of her voice, and when Laurence's hands came on her she screamed as if she was being touched with hot irons.

She still continued to struggle as he carried her up the stairs, followed by the agitated cavalcade of Vance and Sarah Overmeer, and of Kate and MacKay. But when they reached the bedroom and he laid her on the bed and the door was closed on all but him and Aunt Sarah, she knew she was no match for them, and quite suddenly she became still. She even submitted to Sarah pushing three tablets into her mouth and making her swallow some water. Then she closed her eyes to blot out Laurence's gaze, and she began repeating to herself, I loathe you, I loathe you. I do. Not until the sleeping pills began to take effect did the phrase lose its vehemence, but even so it slipped forcefully into her subconscious and laid its indelible print there.

Four

'Speak to me, Bridget.'

'What do you want me to say?'

Sarah Overmeer put her hand across her deep brow and brought it slowly over her eyes, and she kept it there as she said, 'Anything . . . anything . . . only don't sit staring like that all the time . . . I said I'm sorry. We're all sorry to the heart.'

'You're sorry for what I heard, Aunt Sarah, but not for what you intended to do.'

'Don't say that, Bridget.'

'You asked me to speak.'

Sarah Overmeer nodded her head slowly.

'You were quite willing to tie me to Laurence, even when you knew he didn't love me, had never loved me, just to save the firm.'

'Oh, Bridget, what can I say?'

'You could have asked me for the money; wouldn't that have been a better way?'

'You wouldn't have been allowed to part with such a large sum; Grandma would have seen to that.'

'It's my money, not Grandma's. I can do what I like with it.'

'You know nothing about money, child. You don't even know how much you are worth.'

That was true, Bridget thought; she didn't know how much she was worth. Money had no real value to her; she had always had it and her tastes were simple. She had never once in the whole of her life spent her quarterly allowance. She had a private account which, over the years, had accumulated a considerable sum. Now and again when she had thought about money she had given someone a present, such as sending Yvonne a hundred dollars for her birthday. Even her grandmother was money conscious, although in a different way altogether from Aunt Sarah and her household. But now the cards were on the table she could, in a way, feel sorry for Aunt Sarah. But not for Uncle Vance, or Laurence. There was a feeling in her now towards Laurence that terrified her. It had emerged after the long sleep following the hysteria of last night. The sleeping tablets had done their work and she had awakened to the clock striking twelve and the daylight penetrating a chink in the curtains, and as her memory of the previous evening returned there had arisen this feeling, and so strong was it that it had returned her to full consciousness with its force. She had never hated or loathed anyone in her life, there had been no need, but now she was almost consumed with this feeling towards Laurence, and it was fed by one piece of knowledge that stood out from all the rest. It was that he would have married her knowing in his heart that he would return to Mrs Crofton, and that it was impossible for him not to. He would have used her only as a means to support the foundations of a crumbling business.

It seemed as if life had hit her between the eyes, and suddenly given her sight. Yet all the turmoil in her mind now was hiding behind the demeanour of the old Bridget. Although she had spoken plainly to her aunt it had been in the manner of the old Bridget, even though she was no longer the old Bridget. It was as if she were playing a part. She had joined their company and was matching her acting against theirs, yet curiously enough they seemed to have stopped acting; or at least Aunt Sarah had.

Sarah Overmeer was speaking again. She had

asked a question and Bridget gave her an answer. She gave it with one swift movement of her head. Then she said, tensely, 'No, Aunt Sarah, I cannot see Laurence. I will not see him. For the time that I am to remain here it is better that we don't meet.'

'What do you mean, the time that you are to remain here, Bridget?'

'I intend to go to Grandma's tomorrow.'

'That is impossible; you are in no fit state to get up, let alone travel.'

'We will see by tomorrow.' Bridget's voice was even.

'I'll send John in to see you before he leaves; he'll make you see sense in this direction at any rate.'

'Before he leaves?' Bridget pulled herself up in the bed. 'He didn't say he was going anywhere.'

'He wants to do a little fishing before his holiday ends; at least that's what he says. But it wouldn't surprise me if he went straight back to his practice. He's itching to get away. I can always tell. I know John.' Sarah Overmeer stared at Bridget for some moments but said no more. Then, heavily, she rose from her seat and quietly left the room. Her back was slightly stooped and again Bridget's pity was invoked, but she thrust it aside with the thought: She didn't care about what I would go through just as long as I married him, so that this house and all her possessions and her way of life would be secure. Sarah deserved no pity, yet the pity in Bridget remained. But now her mind jumped to John's departure. Why hadn't he told her he was going? She felt panic rising in her. Without John's support she would have to stand alone. Although he had been very offhand with her these past two days he was still John, the only one apart from Grandma on whom she could depend.

Anyway that settled it: she was staying in bed no longer. She had just swung her legs out of the bed and shrugged her arm into her dressing-gown when a knock on the door caused her to call out, 'Come in,' before she realised that it wasn't John's knock and that Kate's tap was but a prelude to the actual opening of the door and the appearance of Laurence.

Her body was rigid as she stared at Laurence, and as her lips parted on an exclamation he raised his hand and said, 'Don't say it. Don't say it.' He was standing with his back to the door now, and she knew that he had spoken to the Bridget he had always known and that he could see her in no other light.

She watched him take slow, heavy strides

towards her, and when he was about a yard from her she said sharply, 'Don't come any nearer, please.'

Her tone caused his eyebrows to rise slightly.

'All right, my dear, I won't contaminate you.'

She walked towards the window and sat down, because she knew that her legs would not support her. She heard him pull a chair forward, and then he was sitting opposite her, leaning forward, his elbows on his knees, his hands clasped lightly together. This brought his face nearer and on a level with her own and she found that her eyes were not avoiding it, but were searching it, searching for something that would show the nature of the man beneath it. But the face betrayed nothing. It still had the attractive charm that had the power to fascinate. But as she continued to stare into Laurence's eyes, she knew that for her his power was dead. Even as short a while ago as yesterday the fascination of him still held her, but not any more; that too had died, had been killed by hearing his voice coming from the study last night. And now a feeling of contempt was added to the new emotions he had created in her. She could at this moment have said what she had to say and so save him the plea he was about to make, but she remained silent, and he began to speak.

'I'm going to make a confession, Bridget.' He waited for some response, but when none was forthcoming he gave a little jerk of his head, then went on. 'I did see Joyce . . . Mrs Crofton, the other evening, but I want you to believe this, and it's true, no matter what you think.' He accompanied the words with quick nods of his head. 'I had no intention of seeing her again. I was taken aback when I found her in the drawing-room, but when I saw her to the door she asked . . . she begged that I meet her later on. She was in great distress. I . . . well, I might as well admit that I was afraid of what she might do or say and so I promised to see her, and there . . .' He now spread out his hands, palms upturned, towards her. 'That's the whole story.'

Bridget was leaning back in her chair and pressing her head into the upholstery, the index finger of her right hand scratching a pattern on the arm, and she heard her voice, which was not really her voice but one like that of a woman, a worldly woman, saying, 'And you have met her a number of times since we became engaged?'

She watched his thick eyelids flick downwards. Then he was looking at her full in the face again. His lips were pressed together, pushing his cheeks up into what could have been taken for a self-conscious smile, but there was no reflection of a smile in his eyes as he answered, 'Yes, I might as well put the cards on the table now that we are at it. Yes, I've seen her a number of times.'

It had been a shot in the dark, for she'd had no foundation for this surmise, and now she found her lips drawing back from her teeth in disgust. The effect was not lost on him and it brought him to his feet, saying, 'I'm a man, Bridget, a man. You were a child, you acted like a child when you should have been a woman; you were old enough but you refused to be wakened, that's the truth of it. You could have kept me tied to you if you had liked. I gave you the opportunity time and time again but you acted like someone who had been born and bred in a convent. But what am I saying? I have known convent-bred girls who were matured women at sixteen. You are twenty-two, Bridget, and you are still clinging to your fairytale world.'

'Not any more, Laurence.'

'What?'

Her tone brought his head thrusting forward.

'I said, not any more.'

'Well, that's something to hear. Perhaps we can talk as two adults now.'

'Yes, Laurence, perhaps we can.' She watched

now as a slow smile spread over his face and, with a quick movement, he resumed his seat. Bending towards her again, he said quietly, 'Give me a chance, Bridget, and I'll prove to you we can make a go of it.'

'You must not have heard me right, Laurence. I said . . . not any more.' She pulled herself up straighter in the chair as if to widen the distance between them, before adding slowly, 'The thought of you touching me turns my stomach, and if you as much as attempt to, I believe I would kill you . . . Yes, that surprises you. Dreamy, far away, pliable Bridget, having the courage to say that. And I *could* kill you, Laurence, just for being what you are, what I couldn't see, what I made myself blind to, for you are mean, ruthless . . . and dirty. Yes, dirty. Dirty in more senses than one, for you would have married me and made my life a hell, just to get your hands on my money, because dear Bridget' – she found she was mimicking her Aunt Sarah's voice now – 'dear Bridget was so bemused and beguiled by dear Laurence that she and her money would be clay in his hands . . . that was it, wasn't it?' They were glaring at each other as she finished, 'And now, get out. Get away from me, for I can't stand the sight of you.'

Laurence's face had turned a deep plum colour and even his eyes were tinted with it. He rose, jerking the chair aside with his feet. Then, after a deep intake of breath, he ground out, 'It's just as well you are who you are or I would . . .'

'What would you do, Laurence?'

He swallowed as he glared down at her, then from deep in his throat he said, 'There're more ways of striking out than with the flat of your hand, and since there's mud flying about and it's all coming in my direction, I think I'm entitled to throw a little back. So we'll now chat about Mr Bruce Dickenson, shall we? You can't tell me what happened the other evening had no precedent, can you? And did I ever throw it at you that you used to go out at night when the house was asleep and meet him, and run wild with him through the woods?'

Bridget found that her mouth and her eyes had stretched simultaneously.

'Yes, that surprises you, doesn't it? Can you deny it?'

'No, and I'm not going to. But it wasn't what you think.'

'Huh!' He sneered down at her. 'Doesn't everybody say that? What proof have you to the contrary? I've only your word for it and I've got as much right to doubt it as you have mine . . .

You look so startled, you're wondering how I know, aren't you? Well, how do I know? Brace yourself . . . Mrs Crofton told me. Yes, that surprises you, doesn't it? It happened that Mr Crofton had seen you on two occasions and naturally he told his wife but, being a gentleman – oh, yes, he's a gentleman – and thinking he saw the same gentlemanly qualities in Bruce Dickenson, he felt no harm would come to you . . . But someone else saw you, too. Who? No other than your rescuer of the other evening, Ryder. And Ryder informed his mistress. But my mother, being a very sensible woman, did not upbraid you; but if you remember you were whisked off to Grandma's. Do you remember? So can you blame me for thinking that whatever happened between you and your friend, Bruce, the other evening was not the first time? You could hardly say you were strangers, could you? Now what have *you* to say, Miss God Almighty?'

It was a few seconds before she answered him, for in spite of her anger she was feeling weak and she found it difficult to keep her voice steady as she said, 'I have nothing to say, except perhaps that I would consider Bruce Dickenson a better man than you could ever hope to be. So now get out. And my last word is that I am leaving here tomorrow and nothing you could say, and no persuasion from Aunt Sarah and Uncle Vance, will make me change my mind. The wedding presents will be returned and a notice put in the papers.'

She had to turn her eyes from his face now, and from the sight of him grinding his large, square, white teeth one across the other. The sound made her flesh creep and his next words brought a tinge of fear to her. 'You said a moment ago you could kill me. Well, the strength of feeling which prompted those words is a mere flea bite to what I am feeling at this moment, for, dear little Bridget Gether, I could quite easily strangle you. Do you hear?' He was hissing at her now. 'I could strangle you!' He glared at her a moment longer before swinging round towards the door. There he stopped and, jerking his head over his shoulder, added, 'As for you running helter-skelter to dear Grandma's, you are going to be disappointed. Father has already left to meet her in London this morning. They should be here this evening. And who knows, when Grandma hears about your little escapade, in her inimitable way, she might think it necessary to persuade you to change your mind. She might think it circumspect that you get married as soon as possible. That being so, you know what my answer would be ... I would laugh in your face. You narrow-minded, suburban little prig.'

The stout door crashed as he banged it behind him. Following a few moments of rigid stillness, Bridget's shoulders slumped and her head drooped onto her chest.

Perhaps she would wake up in a moment and realise she had just experienced a dreadful nightmare. Never since she had first known Laurence had she quarrelled with him; he had at times been angry with her and there had been a coldness separating them, as on the other evening at the pool, but there had never been angry words, or any semblance of a lover's quarrel, for the simple reason that the Bridget she had been wouldn't have dreamed of going against Laurence in any way. She had covered the hurt, bred of the hidden knowledge of Mrs Crofton's place in Laurence's life, with his denial of it. He had denied it simply by saying there was no-one but her now. But looking back, she asked herself how she could have been so childish, so stupid, so gullible as to believe him. The answer was, simply, because she wanted to believe him.

And in this, their first quarrel and their last, she had said she could kill him, and he had said that he would like to strangle her. It didn't seem possible. It must really be a nightmare. She closed her eyes and was on the point of turning her face into the wing of the chair when Laurence's rage-filled voice came to her from the landing, crying, 'You mind your own damn business and you'll have enough to do. You're the one to talk. I don't pick mine from the gutter. As for Joyce, you're green, aren't you? You wanted her yourself but were too frightened of her man to go ahead ... Oh, you can't tell me anything.'

'Doctor! Doctor!' It was MacKay's voice, stern, steadying. Following this there was silence.

Bridget rose slowly to her feet, her eyes on the door. John must have heard them quarrelling and said something to Laurence. It didn't need much to set them at each other's throats. Of a sudden she was attacked by a wave of fear. Fear of Laurence, but not for what he might do to her, but what he might do to John. She couldn't explain the feeling, she only knew she was thankful now that John was leaving today. As for herself, she wouldn't be long after him. Neither Grandma nor anyone else could keep her here now. She paused in her thinking; what did they hope to accomplish by bringing Grandma here? Surely they knew that she was against the lot of them. But perhaps they didn't know. Perhaps that arrogant old lady was the best actor of them all.

Five

Hester Gether was a tall woman. Her frame was ramrod straight and she looked modernly slim. At seventy-nine there was little flesh left under the sagging skin, yet so virile was she still that she could have easily passed, and often did, for a woman in her middle sixties. She was a warm-hearted and astute woman, whose main interest and concern in life was her granddaughter, Bridget. From the moment she arrived at Balderstone twenty-four hours before, she realised that a change had come over the child. She had always thought of her as a child, a trusting, sweet child. That was why she had been so against this marriage, for Laurence, she knew, was not the man to have patience with a child-wife. With some men the task of turning her into a woman would have been a privilege and delight, but she knew Laurence too well to give him the credit for any delicacy. In her own mind she termed Laurence a hog, albeit a charming hog; but she knew it was the charm alone that Bridget had seen, and had been beguiled by.

But now that danger was over, finished. Bridget would never marry Laurence. That being so, her mind should be at rest regarding her, but it wasn't. It was concerned with the fact that she would never be able to think of her as a child any more, for there was no childishness about Bridget now; she had been sprung overnight, as it were, into womanhood. And what had caused this? The business with that young Bruce Dickenson . . . ?

Sarah was positive that the worst had happened there, and judging by Ryder's graphic description, it might well have, for although Bridget maintained firmly, even aggressively, that nothing whatever had happened her changed attitude aroused grave doubts in Hester Gether's mind. Yet, on the other hand, the change wrought in her could have been caused by the knowledge of Laurence's outrageous perfidy. Yes indeed, yes.

The old lady was sitting at the study window and looking across the sunless garden down towards the rowan walk. Shelving the matters that were foremost in her mind she said, 'There's hardly a berry left on the rowans; the birds have been having a feast. It's always puzzled me why they don't pick them up from the ground. The ground can be smothered with berries but they take flying darts at a branch that is too slender to hold them and don't stop until they've stripped it; yet by standing on their feet they could have had their fill. It has always intrigued me.'

Bridget was sitting and looking into the coal fire which Hester Gether always insisted on no matter how warm the day, and when she made no answer, her grandmother went on, 'Winter will soon be upon us again. Oh, I have always hated northern winters.'

'How soon can we go, Grandma?'

Hester did not turn her head but her eyes roamed the wide stretch of sky as she answered, 'John says tomorrow or the next day . . . He is not so much thinking of you now as of me. I am past doing return trips non-stop. I'll see how I feel tomorrow. I'll make it as soon as I can, for then he will accompany us back, at least as far as London. It was more than good of him to put off his departure because of me. But then John was always considerate.' She brought her eyes from the sky and looked down at her hands and sat silently musing as if her thoughts were on the man she had been talking about.

'Has the notice gone into the papers, Grandma?'

'Yes. Yes, it has.'

'You're sure?'

'Child, I've told you it has.'

'What did it say?'

Hester turned her gaze from Bridget's enquiring eyes; then she sighed deeply before answering, 'Sarah insisted that it say the wedding was postponed because of your illness. Now don't worry, don't worry.' She put her hand out reassuringly towards Bridget. 'They know as well as we do there'll be no wedding, but I had to let her have her own way in this, for it softened the blow somewhat. Your Aunt Sarah was always one for prestige; she cannot bear to think of the county reaction. Because it was to be quite an affair, wasn't it? I'm very sorry for you, my dear, you know that.' She leant forward and patted Bridget's cheek as she smiled sadly. 'But I'm sorry for Sarah too; I've never been much in sympathy with her but she's going through a pretty bad time at present.'

'It's the money she's worried about, not the wedding.' Bridget's voice was harsh.

'Yes, in a way you're right there, I think.'

'Well, she can have it—' She was making this generous statement in the same harsh tone when her words were cut off by her grandmother exclaiming, 'What! Oh no, she can't. Not if I still have anything to do with it. And since you're not married I still have a say in your affairs. This new factory is a shot in the dark, and a bad shot, to my way of thinking: there's too much competition in that line already. Your money isn't inexhaustible, my dear, and what you have would be swallowed up in the first effort to get the place going.'

'Well, what odds? The money doesn't matter to me.'

'No, it doesn't because you have it. Most young people with money talk like you do because they haven't had the experience of being without money. Don't you undervalue money, Bridget, or you'll make the biggest mistake of your life.'

'You don't take that attitude with John.' Bridget looked sharply at her grandmother. 'When you knew he was spending his last on other people you said he was casting his bread upon the waters.'

'Yes, I did, because John was helping individuals, people in need; and besides, he's a man with a profession and can make more, whereas if you had to earn your living you'd be hard put to it . . . Oh, I know all about your painting, but artists are ten a penny in the labour market, so you take care; and what is more, take an interest in your money, for you'll need it, you'll see. But if you let Vance get his hands on it, it'll be good-bye, for he's up to his neck in debt on the old factory, and if he couldn't make a go of that, what chance will he have with a new one? All this talk of wider horizons and competing abroad is wishful thinking. I would be the first one to say advance, go ahead, and take a share in the new venture if he had made a go of the old one, but Vance, up till two years ago, thought of nothing but himself and his pleasures and how lavishly he could entertain. And he didn't stop until the debts were up to his neck and nearly drowning him. Since which time he has tried to swim, but when he found it impossible, you, my dear, were to act as a lifebuoy. But in my opinion, he was too far sunk for any lifebuoy to be of much assistance . . . And, by the way, that, my dear, is what I wanted to tell you when you came to me six months ago, but you seemed,' – she paused – 'you seemed so set on the marriage, so mad about Laurence, that I thought you would have your own way in any case, no matter what happened, so I kept quiet. At least,

I did to you, but not to Laurence. They all knew what I thought, but if, my dear, I had said to you, "It's your money they're after," what would have been your reaction?'

Bridget's head was bowed low now, and she replied, 'I don't know. I only know that although I feel bitter inside and boiled up about . . . about everything, I still don't want to see them bankrupt; everything would go.'

The old lady leant forward and took Bridget's hand between her thin bony ones, and straightening out the nervous plucking fingers, she stroked them soothingly as she said, 'That's not your worry, my dear. And it's ten to one that even if you had married and they had used your money, even then it would only be a matter of time. At least, that's how I feel. I felt so strongly about this, Bridget, that I made a new will. What I have is shared between you and Yvonne, as you know, but what is coming to you I put into trust and you will receive it as an allowance. I wanted to make sure that you had something.'

'Oh, Grandma . . . Grandma.' Bridget rose and put her arm around the old lady's shoulder and, bringing her head to rest on her breast, she whispered brokenly, 'What would I do without you? There's no-one in this wide world that cares a hoot about me, but you.'

'Tut. Tut. Nonsense. John thinks the world of you.'

'Sometimes.'

'What do you mean, sometimes?'

'Oh, he's been like a bear with a sore skull since he got better. I've never known him so bad-tempered.'

'John bad-tempered with you . . .? You must have dreamt it, child.'

'I didn't dream it. Yesterday he was prepared to leave me here on my own, knowing how I felt after Laurence and I had that frightful row, and he would have gone if you hadn't insisted on his staying.'

'Me, insist?' The old lady bridled now. 'I did nothing of the kind: it was his own idea. I never said a word . . .'

'You don't have to, Grandma.' Bridget smiled weakly. 'And all right, you didn't insist.'

'All I said was, I wanted to talk to him, and about something important, and it is important . . . It's about a new practice. I've got the very place for him. I'm all for helping suffering humanity, but you can do it without living in the deep slums. This self-sacrificing attitude is a form of conceit with him. I've told him before now that what he's got to do is to get a practice out of that place. So I have been looking into it;

I have a number of friends, you know, in that line.'

The faint smile spread slightly. 'Yes, I know, Grandma, and John knows too.' Then, the smile disappearing, she added, 'But Aunt Sarah isn't pleased at him staying on. She almost said so to his face last night.'

'Well—' The old lady's eyebrows moved up into two thin points. 'I don't suppose his visit is very welcome at this time.'

'Why not?'

'Oh well, there are reasons.'

'But what reasons could there be, Grandma? She used to like John staying here.'

'Well, we won't go into it at the present moment; perhaps some time later, eh?' She leant forward and patted Bridget's hand and was about to say something further when the door opened and Sarah Overmeer, her face white and set, entered the room. She stood for a moment looking at the old lady before she said stiffly, 'There is someone wishing to speak to you on the phone.' She deliberately did not look at Bridget.

'Me? Who is it?' Hester turned her head to look at her stepdaughter as she spoke. 'Can't Frances deal with it?'

'Frances is out in the grounds at the moment:

she wanted a breath of air.' Sarah spoke as if the old lady was in the habit of restricting her maid-companion's activities even to the extent of depriving her of fresh air.

'Well, I hope she gets plenty of it.' With this caustic remark Hester cast a quick, quizzical glance at Bridget, then rising slowly from the chair, she left the room and followed her step-daughter into the hall, leaving the door open behind her.

Bridget watched the straight back of Sarah Overmeer as she crossed the hall, and in spite of everything she knew about her, in spite of the limits that her aunt would have gone to to make her own life secure, she could not help but be concerned for her. She saw her as a victim of a long and unhappy marriage and the mother of a son who was but the replica of his father. But whereas she might feel sorry for her, her feeling of hatred towards Laurence had if anything deepened in intensity, and to such an extent that she was beginning to hate herself for her un-compromising attitude. The memory of their last meeting was still vividly with her. She could still hear her own high-pitched voice spitting out her anger. It was a disconcerting revelation to know that she could be so strong in her passion, so vehement in her dislike as to want to kill the man she had, up to a few days ago, loved, worshipped even.

'You must not have him here.' The high, angry voice of Sarah Overmeer broke in upon Bridget's thoughts.

'If you won't allow him into your house, my dear Sarah, then all there is left to me is to stay somewhere else in the village and he can come to me there.'

'What if Vance or Laurence comes in? There'll be murder done.'

'Don't make me laugh, Sarah. Vance's courage is all in his tongue and it's not very convincing at that. As for Laurence, it is Bruce Dickenson that he would like to murder, not his father, and it is his father who has asked to come and speak to me . . . and Bridget . . . And by the way, Sarah, the man says he sent a letter by hand to Bridget yesterday. Do you know anything about it?'

A silence followed this query, and it was her grandmother's voice that Bridget heard again, saying quietly, 'You are not a really clever woman, Sarah, you never were. Ruthless, but not clever. I could almost say I hate people who interfere with private mail.'

'Without that reason, you have always hated me.'

'That is not true, Sarah, and you know it. You

159

resented me from the moment I married your father. You made it plain that this could never be my home and I never considered it my home, but hate you or bear you any ill-will, never. This house, I could say, has been your downfall, although you consider it evidence of your prestige. If you had thought more of Vance instead of this ugly stone box, your life would have been happier and you might even have prevented the present financial chaos . . . But we're getting down to personalities. To get back to the subject that matters most at the moment, Mr Dickenson will be here just as quickly as it takes his car to cover the distance. If Vance or Laurence should come in while he is in the house, you can tell them that I overrode your orders.'

When Hester Gether entered the room she paused for a moment after closing the door behind her, and as she walked forward she looked hard at Bridget and stated, 'You heard all that?'

'Yes, Grandma.'

'Well, then,' – the tone was crisp – 'there's no need to go into it all again.'

'But . . . but what does Mr Dickenson want?'

'I don't really know, except perhaps to apologise for his son's behaviour.'

'There's no need.' Bridget bit on her thumb-nail. 'Why keep it up?'

'That's beside the point, child. Henry Dickenson wants to do the right thing. He's an upright man, as was his father and grandfather. In fact, I would go as far as to say that they had more true breeding in them than anyone who was born in this house. I don't know much about the young Bruce, but you say yourself he always acted very well towards you; until that one instance, and then you say he was drunk. If at one time you ran wild in the woods with him and you came to no harm . . .' The old lady held up her hand in a warning gesture. 'Oh, I know all about it, I've been given the full story, and if that is so, the man has some good in him. And you would have gone on being aware of nothing but good had he not been to a wedding, as you yourself told me, and drank too much. Now the position is this: Mr Dickenson wishes to speak to you. He is greatly troubled, I understand. I also understand that he sent you a note yester-day and phoned a number of times. It was Mrs Dickenson who asked to speak to me just now, and I doubt, had Sarah recognised her voice, the message would have ever reached me. Immediately she heard me speak she put her hus-band on the phone. It's coming to something, isn't it, when people have to sink to subterfuge to speak to me. And now I suppose I'll have to go and find Frances and get her to await his arrival, in case Sarah instructs Ryder to send the man packing.'

'Let *me* go, Grandma. I want to do something. I'll go mad just sitting here.'

'I think, my dear, it would be advisable if you kept yourself in the background until we leave. You don't want to go bumping into any one of them, do you? You never know what it might lead to, because tempers are pretty high at present. No, I'll see Frances and I'll try to locate John and bring him back with me. He can be amusing at times.'

'Not any more.'

The old lady glanced at her granddaughter, then shook her head before exclaiming, 'As you've said, I think the sooner you get away from here the better. You're colouring everyone with the same brush.'

Half an hour later Frances, a comely, homely-looking woman in her thirties, tapped on the study door and announced Mr Dickenson.

Mr Dickenson, unlike his son, was a man well over six feet in height. His body was sparse of flesh and hard and straight, and he looked a man of dignity, a straightforwardly honest man. He inclined his head towards the old lady as he said, 'Good morning, Mrs Gether.'

'Good morning, Mr Dickenson.' Hester accompanied her words with a movement of her heavily ringed hand, then added, 'Take a seat, Mr Dickenson.'

'Thank you.' When he was seated, Mr Dickenson looked towards Bridget for the first time and said quietly, 'I hope you feel better, miss . . . I . . . didn't expect to be able to see you.'

Before Bridget could answer, her grandmother put in, 'But that's what you wished, wasn't it, Mr Dickenson?'

'Yes, definitely.' He looked at the old lady, then turned his gaze again towards Bridget. 'I wanted to have a word with you. Are you well enough to hear me?'

'Yes, yes, of course, Mr Dickenson.' Bridget's voice was low and steady. 'But I can assure you there's no need to say anything.'

'I think there is, miss. Well, first of all I would say that my . . . my son is in great distress of mind and physically in a bad way. He did not return home till dawn following the . . . the incident. He had been lying in the wood and had lost a great deal of blood, and if it hadn't been for the doctor coming quickly on the scene, it might have been very serious. But all this doesn't wipe out what happened, what he did. I am not making excuses for that.' He turned his gaze fully towards the old lady as if to add weight to this statement, before going on, 'But my son is a good man, miss; I've never known him to be the worse for drink before. He can take and hold a little like any ordinary fellow, but he drank more than was good for him that day because he was distressed; he was distressed about you, miss. He was concerned for your happiness, *your* happiness not his own, and I want you to believe that, because some long time ago he had faced up to the fact that you were not for him. I might as well tell you, miss, that I did not agree with him on that point. You might have more money than he has, but when it comes to heritage and breeding he could definitely compare favourably with anything you had to offer.' Again his gaze flashed towards the old lady, and he added quickly, 'I am not meaning to insult, madam, you understand that?'

'I understand you, Mr Dickenson. Go on.'

Mr Dickenson was again holding Bridget's attention, and he went on, 'My son was in love with you, deeply in love with you, but he considered you not only above him socially but . . . well . . . well, more of a child. A child who trusted him, and he acted accordingly. If he had taken my advice he would have declared his feelings and run off with you. Yes,' – his head moved downwards – 'yes, that's what I advised, and I would like to wager you would have been much happier today if he had taken that advice . . . And now we come to the other night. I don't know what happened, and he remembers only vaguely, but he remembers . . .' He paused now and removing his gaze from Bridget, he looked down as he said, 'He remembers trying to make love to you and you resisting him strongly, and then something hit him on the back of the head. When he came to he was alone in the hut and knew he must get away. He let himself down the face of the rock. How he managed that, he cannot remember, either. And then he reached the wood. It was hours before he was himself again, at least before he could remember, even vaguely, what had happened, and since then he has been like a man demented. He wrote to you, and when he received no answer to his letter he begged me to phone. He wanted to come and see you and to tell you . . . that he is not sorry you are no longer going to marry Mr Overmeer, for both he and I know that was the best possible thing that could have happened to you. I am sorry if I am hurting you by saying this, miss, and you, ma'am.' He again cast a glance in Hester's direction. 'But the future will prove the truth of it. But what he also sent me to say was what he would have said himself if he was allowed entry into this house, or if you would have seen him, as he asked in the letter. That he is sorry to the soul of him for forcing himself on you, for frightening you, because that is what he remembers clearly: your terror and his ignoring of it. Even if you say you forgive him, miss, I know that he will never forgive himself . . . And now may I ask you something as a great, great favour to me?'

Bridget could not help but be deeply affected by the sincerity of this man, who was but an older replica of Bruce. She said gently, 'Go on, Mr Dickenson.'

'Well, it is this, miss. When you are well enough, would you see him? Would you let him speak to you? I think this, and only this, will end the turmoil that is in his mind. I repeat that my son is a good man, yes, and his love for you was a good thing. If he doesn't have peace of mind he will be destroyed. He has never been a man for the women. Like me, he has been singular in his purpose. This, perhaps, makes us a little narrow in our judging of others. Be that as it may, what answer am I to give him?'

Bridget, lifting her eyes from the contemplation of her hands, and looking straight at Mr Dickenson, said, 'I'm ... we are leaving here tomorrow and there won't be time to see him, but tell him that of course I will later, and tell him ... tell him not to worry any more, Mr Dickenson. I understand, and I do know' – she nodded her head to emphasise her words – 'it would never have happened if he hadn't been drunk. I know that.'

'Thank you, miss, I'll tell him. It will certainly ease his mind ... And about your arm, miss, I understand it's broken.'

'Oh, no, no, it's not broken, Mr Dickenson. It just slipped its socket. It's all right now.'

'Well that will be some source of relief anyway. And now I won't detain you any longer.' He rose to his feet, then turning to Hester Gether, he said, 'It's a pity you ever left this house, ma'am.'

The old lady, with a characteristic gesture, pushed her eyebrows up towards her white hair. 'Thank you for the thought, Mr Dickenson, but it remains a matter of opinion.'

Mr Dickenson was again looking at Bridget, and she was waiting for him to speak when her attention was lifted to a movement outside the door. She glanced towards it and heard Kate's flurried voice exclaiming, 'They're . . . they're in the study, Doctor.' The next moment the door opened and John entered.

'Oh, I'm sorry . . . I didn't know . . .' He stopped and Hester exclaimed, 'Oh, come away in; you don't need any introduction to Mr Dickenson, I'm sure.'

'No, no, I don't that.' John smiled towards the older man and Mr Dickenson's countenance brightened, 'Good day, Doctor.'

'Good day, Mr Dickenson.'

'I was just off.'

'Now don't go because of me.'

'No, no, I won't, Doctor, but my errand's finished. So,' he turned towards Hester, 'good day, ma'am, and thank you.'

'Good day, Mr Dickenson, and thank you for coming.'

'Good day, Miss Bridget.'

'Good day, Mr Dickenson, and . . . tell Bruce it's all right.'

'Thank you, miss. Thank you indeed.'

After the door had closed on Mr Dickenson, John did not ask, Why was he here and how on earth did he get in?, which would have been only natural. Nor did Hester Gether give any explanation. Instead, pointedly ignoring the subject, she smiled widely up at him as she said,

'Come and sit down and tell me something amusing, something funny.'

John's eyes crinkled and his mouth went into a wry grin as he repeated, 'Something funny, now let's see.' He cupped his chin in the palm of his hand and thought for a moment before asking, 'Do you want it funny ha-ha, or funny peculiar?'

'Ha-ha.'

'Ha-ha. You would. Well, I'm sorry, old lady, but I'm short of ha-has at the moment.' He sat down beside her and with his back half-turned towards Bridget.

He seemed to be ignoring Bridget, for he had not even looked at her from the moment he entered the room and his attitude was incensing her. Why had his manner changed towards her all in a matter of two days? What had she done? She was in trouble and if ever she needed his kindness and consideration, it was now. She could see how her grandmother pooh-poohed the idea of any change in him, for with her he was still his playful self. The old lady was saying to him now, 'Are you sure you're really feeling better? Flu, real influenza can take it out of you, and it often leaves a weakness.'

Bridget watched him straighten up and thump his chest with his hand. 'Listen! Sound as a bell,' he said. 'I had an overhaul yesterday and the village crock . . . I mean doc, said, back to work. But take plenty of recreation, he said. Something different from your easy London life. Navvying, he said, would be fine. What you want, John, he said, is a few weekends with a gang of Irish navvies. Digging drains, preferably. It would give you both mental and physical upliftment.'

'Don't be a fool, John.'

'It's true, Grandma.'

'But you're not starting work yet?'

'Next week, as ever was, old lady.'

'Not if I know anything about it. We'll talk about this later. I've got a lot to say to you.'

'Somehow I thought you had.'

As they both laughed, Bridget rose to her feet. Their apparent indifference to her feelings and presence, not to mention their jocularity, was hurting her, but it was also angering her. She felt that more than ever now they were treating her like a young girl, when it must be apparent to both of them that she was no longer the girl of three days ago.

'Bridget?' John was on his feet. 'Where are you going?'

'To my room . . . Why?' she asked the question coldly.

'No reason.' His voice was soft, his manner

was soft. 'Don't be long. We'll take a walk.'

'I don't feel like walking.' She could be awkward, too.

'Don't be silly, child.' Hester Gether's voice was airy and its implication was just too much for Bridget.

'Don't call me a child, Grandma ... Don't ever again call me a child.' She was leaning forward, her voice low and angry. 'I'm twenty-two and I'm having an experience not given to children.'

If Hester Gether was taken aback she did not show it. She looked squarely at her granddaughter for a moment, then turned towards the table and picked up her embroidered bag. But when Bridget swung round towards the door and John made a move towards her, her hand went out and silently stopped him from following her.

When Bridget reached her room her anger had fled and she was aghast at having spoken to her beloved grandmother in such a fashion. For about fifteen minutes she fought with herself; she must go and apologise, she must. She was actually at the door when she heard her Aunt Sarah's voice from the landing saying, 'I told you how it would be; that man should never have been allowed in the house.' Then her grandmother's voice came to her, high and disdainful. 'Well, he was. But what I want to know is, how you come by your knowledge of what he said. Were you listening at the keyhole?'

'How dare you!'

'Oh, I dare, all right, Sarah; don't forget I know you. But if you weren't listening you must have put Kate on duty; she's got very long lobes has that frustrated lady. And don't deny the obvious. If you weren't informed in some way, how were you to know that Bruce Dickenson wanted to meet Bridget, eh? Answer me that.'

There followed a short silence before Sarah Overmeer's voice, cold and cutting now, said, 'My answer to you is that this is *my* house. I have never denied you its doors, but once you are gone this time, I will thank you not to return.'

'Don't worry, Sarah, once I am gone from it this time, as you so pedantically put it, I shall not return. We will likely all be on our way tomorrow . . . John, too.'

'Oh, no doubt, no doubt John will be accompanying you. Of course, you don't want any scandal, do you, and it's so convenient to have a doctor in the family . . . You would even let him risk his reputation to save her, wouldn't you?'

'Be quiet, Sarah!' The old lady's voice sounded

terrible, even terrifying. 'You are out of your mind; this business has unhinged you.'

'Not quite, Hester, and don't think you can put the fear of God into me, because you can't. And now let me tell you why the reason I'm intending to give for the marriage being broken off will be the true one. I'm not going to let Laurence take the brunt of this, no matter what he's done. I'm going to say to anyone who cares to listen that she was having an affair with Bruce Dickenson . . . and of course time, I feel sure, will prove my words.'

'You poor crippled soul.' Bridget could scarcely hear her grandmother's words now. 'I could feel sorry for you, Sarah, for you know in your heart that Laurence is no good. You know that to all intents and purposes he has broken up the Crofton home, and that Bridget found out his latest escapade, which of course wouldn't have been his last with that lady . . . And who was it before her? A young woman in Cambridge. You had a visit from her father, if I remember rightly. But I needn't go on. As I said, Sarah, I'm sorry for you . . . Now kindly move out of my way. I want to enter my room.'

There followed a silence that seemed to vibrate. Bridget waited a few minutes longer before opening the door, then she went out and towards her grandmother's room, which was the last room along the passage leading from the landing. But she was only halfway across the landing when she was brought to a stiff halt by a door opening behind her and a voice exclaiming, 'Well! Well!'

She turned slowly and saw Laurence. He was in his shirt-sleeves; it was a silk shirt and his bulky chest muscles were pressing hard against the material. Bridget noted this, for her eyes were on his chest and not his face. Her legs felt weak, and the weakness was travelling swiftly up her body as she went to turn from him. But his voice held her, saying, 'Wait. Oh wait. Don't deprive me of this small pleasure; I didn't ever expect to see you again. You were to keep to your room until such time as you were fit to depart. But you are looking radiant. Who has performed the miracle? Ah, yes, yes.' He raised his hand, his forefinger pointing upwards, the gesture ludicrously like that of a bishop bestowing a blessing. 'Jonathan! Jonathan, the miracle worker, or is he just the English Dr Kildare? Ah, there . . . there lies the point. Anyway, he has got you onto your feet, and we are grateful, aren't we? At least I am.'

Bridget was forced now to look fully at Laurence, and she saw to her consternation that he was drunk; not drunk in the way Bruce had been, his body rolling and his voice thick; no, Laurence had always been able to carry his drink. The evidence of his indulgence was betrayed only by his eyes: it was as if they were covered by an opaque skin. Once before she had seen his eyes like this, one New Year's Eve, and as the glaze had deepened, so his manner had become more aggressive. But this was not New Year's Eve, this was twelve o'clock noon. It was unheard of that either he or his father took a drink before the lunch aperitif but he must have been drinking heavily for some time. She knew that the best thing to do was to ignore his taunts and get to her grandmother's room as quickly as possible. But as she turned in the direction of the door he was facing her again. With an agility surprising in one so heavily built, he had leapt in front of her.

'Don't leave me like this, Bridget. This might be our last meeting.' His voice was mockingly tender.

'Get out of my way, Laurence; I'm going to Grandma.'

'She is going to Grandma.' He nodded his head first to the right and then to the left as if he were addressing an audience. 'Did you hear that? She is going to Grandma. Tut, tut! How can you suggest she has come out of hibernation to meet Mr Bruce Dickenson? How can you suggest such a thing?' He now, with exaggerated mimicry, put his head on one side and his hand to his ear as if he were listening for an answer. Then went on in indignant tones, 'Because his father came and arranged it? Oh, you have a bad mind.'

Now his eyes returned to Bridget's and he repeated, 'They have bad minds, haven't they, to think that you are going to meet dear Bruce?'

'You're drunk and you're . . . you're horrible.'

'Horrible, am I?' His tone was now thick with bitterness. 'Horrible, she says. All right, have it I'm horrible, but at least I know what I am, whereas you, you sanctimonious little hypocrite, playing the naive child, while all the time . . .' His hands came forward and as they gripped her arms she cried out, as much with pain as with fright: 'Leave go! Leave go! I'll . . . I'll . . .'

'Let her go.' The command was terse, yet quiet, and Laurence, turning his head, looked towards the stairs where stood John, and sent forth a sardonic laugh. He now loosened his hold on Bridget with one hand but held onto her with the other, and as she swung round and strained from him, John, now only about three yards from them, again said, 'Let her go!'

'In my own good time, Doctor.'

'Now!'

Bridget stopped straining from Laurence and became still. She was suddenly overwhelmed with fear, not for herself but for John. This seemed to be the outcome of the premonition she had had the other evening. Yet this was a John she hadn't seen before: this man looked like a wild cat ready to spring. But what chance had he against Laurence on the strength of his bulk alone? She heard herself shout, 'Don't, John!' and at the same moment she was aware of a succession of events. As John's fist shot out with surprising swiftness and caught Laurence on the side of the face, she felt herself hurled against the wall, and then there was commotion all around her. First Grandma's voice was crying, 'What is this? What is this?' And then Kate's voice shouting, 'Now, Doctor . . . sir! Mr Laurence!' Following this there was a second of quietness that held no movement, each person on the landing remaining quite still. John was now standing against the opposite wall near a pedestal that held a bronze urn. Laurence was some yards from it, his arms hanging forward, his whole body in a crouching position. Then movement was set in motion again by Grandma, her voice commanding, 'No more of this! No more of this!'

Bridget's mouth was open and her hand was covering it as she looked at John, who was now standing like a man at bay. She knew that he realised just what kind of a position he was in. If Laurence hit him with his great fist and then hit him again, as he certainly would once he felt the contact of flesh, then it would go hard with him. For, in spite of what he had said, he was not fully recovered from his illness, and had he himself been attending a patient in a similar condition he would, at this stage, have insisted on rest and convalescence.

Horrified and fascinated, Bridget now watched him move his arm sideways until his hand came in contact with the top of the urn, then he gripped it. All this was done without moving his eyes from Laurence. The urn was an ugly piece of art, being made entirely of an entwined serpent – the tail balancing the foot of the urn while the body coiled upwards. The open mouth of the reptile formed the top, its lolling tongue making a lip that came to a point. The urn was eighteen inches high, and heavy. She now watched John gripping it between his hands, one at its base and one in the middle. Then, as Laurence launched at him, one arm outstretched, the fist doubled, John jerked himself sideways and back, and raising the urn above his head he levelled it towards Laurence.

It all happened in a matter of seconds. A concerted horrified cry filled the landing, followed by a momentary stillness as they all looked to where Laurence was spreadeagled against the wall, his body leaning over at an angle. The urn was lying to the side of him, having missed his head by about a foot, but the lip had buried itself in the large portrait hanging at eye level on the wall. It was a portrait of Vance Overmeer in his youth, disfigured now by a gash under the ribs.

Bridget had not previously been aware of Sarah Overmeer's presence on the landing but she now saw her springing forward to where Laurence stood, and as she held onto his arm she glared ferociously at John, crying, 'You maniac! You could have killed him.'

Bridget's hands had slipped down to her throat, the pressure of her fingers almost stopping her breathing. She was waiting for the next move, but none came. She looked across at Laurence. His face, from being red, was now grey. He had received a shock; it would appear he had underestimated the resourcefulness of his opponent. Perhaps this fact penetrated his fuddled brain because, although he pushed off his mother's hands, he made no further attempt to carry on with the fight.

Bridget pulled herself from the wall as she heard her grandmother say, 'Come . . . come, John. Do you hear?'

John seemed slightly dazed and he shook his head as Bridget, now urging herself forward, added her plea to her grandmother's command, saying, 'Please, John, come away . . . please.'

Between them now he walked down the corridor and into Hester Gether's room. Inside, the old lady took charge. 'Get on the bed there and lie down.' She thrust him forward, but he slowly and gently resisted her, saying, 'I'm all right, there's nothing wrong, I'm all right.'

'You're shaking . . . you're shaking like a leaf. There'll be repercussion from this, mark my words. What possessed you to get into a fight with that hulking animal?'

'It was my fault, Grandma.'

Bridget moved away and sat down by the fire. 'I was coming across to see you, and Laurence came out of his room. He had hold of me when John came upstairs.'

'I told you it would be better if you kept out of everyone's way, didn't I? You should have either stayed in the study or in your room.'

'Don't blame her, Grandma.' John seated himself in an armchair to the other side of the fireplace, and leaning his head back, he closed his eyes. Then with a sudden movement he was sitting upright again. Breathing heavily, he drew his hand over his face from the brow to the chin as if trying to wipe something away, and he was almost gasping for breath as he said, 'She was right. Aunt Sarah was right: I might have killed him.'

'Well, you didn't, and don't think any more about it.'

'But I might have.' He was staring up at the old lady, the sweat running down his face. 'I knew the way I was feeling I didn't stand a chance if we came to grips. I . . . I felt I had to do something, but . . . to throw the urn! If that lip had hit him it could have caught him in the eye or the temple . . . my God!' He now dropped his head forward and rested it on his hands.

'Now, now. Don't give way like that, John . . . Come on. Come on. What we want, I think, is a strong cup of tea. Where is Frances? She's never here when she's wanted. Tut, tut! You'd think that woman had never seen a garden in her life. I'll ring for Kate.'

Almost at the same moment as the old lady pressed the bell, the door was thrust open, and simultaneously their heads were jerked in its direction to see Sarah Overmeer. Her face was livid with anger and she was staring, not at John, nor at her stepmother, but at Bridget, and it was to Bridget she spoke. 'I hope you're satisfied, miss, with the devastation you have created in this house. And since you are leaving, I would be happy if you would make it as soon as possible.'

The door closed as quickly as it had opened, and Bridget, looking at Hester Gether, exclaimed, 'Oh, Grandma!'

'Don't worry, my dear, don't worry. But that's settled it, we'll go tomorrow, first thing in the morning. It's too late to start now. It would mean getting into London very late and staying in an hotel: it would be too much for me. No, we'll leave early in the morning. Right, John?'

'Yes.' John had risen to his feet. He was still breathing heavily. 'The quicker we are gone the better.'

'As you say, the quicker the better, and I hope I never look upon this house again. This house doesn't like me, it never has, and it likes neither of you either.' The old lady looked tenderly from one to the other. 'It's managed to break both your lives.'

Bridget knew that, in a way, her life had been broken in this house, yet she could not think of anything that had happened to John to make her grandmother imagine that his life too had been influenced or broken here. Yet it wasn't, as

Grandma said, the house that had the power to break people's lives, it was the people in it; she did not question her grandmother's statement, it wasn't the time for probing.

Hester Gether was saying now, 'I'll send Frances to help you with your packing, Bridget. And you, John, should go and lie down. I'll see that Nancy sends up a tray.'

'No, no. Don't do that. I'll drive into the village and have a bite there.' John inhaled deeply and looked about him in a dazed fashion.

'I wouldn't risk going out if I were you. Look,' she pointed to the window, 'it's quite black over Mickle Fell. There's a storm brewing up.'

'Well, I'd rather face the storm outside than the one in. Don't worry. I'll be all right.' He was about to leave the room when he turned to Bridget and said, 'Do what Grandma suggests: stay in your room until the morning. You will, eh?'

Without waiting for her answer, he went hastily from the room, and the old lady, slowly lowering herself into a chair, looked at the closed door and remarked, 'It was right what he said: he could have killed him and in that moment of time I've never seen a man more determined to do just that.'

Bridget shivered, a visible shiver. Quietly she

said, 'I'm going to start packing, Grandma,' and left the room.

When she reached her room she stood with her back to the door, chiding herself for scurrying across the landing like a frightened rabbit. And she told herself, so much for her changed personality. Yet who could blame her for being frightened, for there was something in the house to be afraid of. She could feel it all around her, tangible, like solidified hate.

Six

The storm broke at around three o'clock. like
the atmosphere in the house, the air had been
heavy all afternoon; the sky became so low at
one point that it seemed to be resting on the
actual fells, or touching the treetops, lying there,
still and waiting, not making enough movement
to stir a blade of grass, awaiting, as it were, the
summons to attack.

And when the storm did break it came in the
form of an attack. Up through the valley came a
great rush of wind, bending all before it. Its
objective seemed to be Balderstone, for it
battered the house as if determined to level
it. There was no rain for some time and when
eventually it did start its arrival was slow. Large
wide-spaced drops pinged intermittently at the
windows for some time; then, as if tired of being

playful, they combined to form a steel sheet which threatened to force its way through the great stones of the house.

When the rain first started Bridget and Frances were packing and Bridget's mind was too preoccupied to take much notice, until later it was forced upon her that what was pounding the house was no ordinary rain, it was a deluge. At the window she could see nothing outside but the rain itself being driven almost horizontally over the fells, and as she watched it she thought it was as if the weather was attacking something equally wild within the house.

But the packing was finished now and there was nothing more to do . . . but sit. She looked about her, thinking she would go mad if she had to stay in this room until the morning. What was more she wasn't going to; and why should she, anyway? She began to feel indignant. Her Aunt Sarah was blaming her for all that had happened, when the truth of the matter was Sarah Overmeer herself was the instigator of it all. And she would tell her so; yes, she would if she as much as spoke one more word of blame, she would turn on her. She had stood enough, quite enough.

The Grandma Gether trait emerging well to the fore now, she went boldly out and once again, crossing the landing – not hurrying this time – tapped on her grandmother's door. In a second it was opened by Frances with her finger to her lips. 'Ssh! she's asleep,' she said.

'Oh.' Bridget felt slightly deflated. 'I . . . I wanted to tell her I'm going down to the study.'

'I'll tell her when she wakes.'

'Thanks, Frances,' she whispered in reply.

Frances smiled, nodded her head, then closed the door, leaving Bridget standing as if she was alone in a strange place. She felt lost and undecided about what to do. Should she go downstairs? Why not? Why not? But John had said . . . Oh, John! It was all right for him; he could get into the car and go for a drive. Was he still out in this? Surely not. Anyway, she could go to his room and tell him she was going down to the study.

When she knocked on the door his voice came to her immediately, calling, 'Yes, come in.'

'Oh.' The exclamation hadn't much welcome in it. He turned in his chair from a little table at which he had been writing, then said, 'I thought the idea was to stay put.'

'I'll go mad staying in my room by myself. I'm going downstairs; that's all I came to say, so I won't disturb you.'

'Don't be silly. Come here.' He held out his

hand, which she didn't take. Instead, she said, slowly, 'Why have you changed so these past few days?'

'Changed? I haven't changed.'

'Oh, don't hedge, John. You used to like me coming in and talking; we've always talked. My conversation might not have been very intellectual, but up till recently it didn't bore you; at least, if it did, you were good at pretending – but now . . . you . . . you are not only offhand, you actually shun me. What have I done?'

'Oh, Bridget.' He stopped and stared at her, then reaching out, he took her hand. 'I'm sorry. I didn't mean to appear like that, and I promise you one thing: once we are gone from here I'll be different.'

'Once we leave here you won't have to bother about being different, because we won't see much of each other, will we?'

He looked into her eyes, eyes that had expressed little sadness or trouble during the course of her life. Now, sadness and trouble went far into their depths. It was some time before he gave a reply to her statement, and then he said, 'Wait and see.' He smiled now. 'Your life may be so full in the future that you'll even forget the last time you saw me.'

'Don't be silly. I always feel you are covering

up something when you talk like that,' she said. 'You're not looking too good. Why don't you lie down?'

'It wouldn't be a bad idea.' He looked towards the window. 'Can't do much on a day like this; outside, I mean. I was lucky. I just got back from the village before it broke.'

'Did you have a good lunch?'

'Passable. But I wasn't hungry . . . Well.' He smiled at her. 'I'll finish this letter, then I'll do what nurse orders and lie down for an hour.'

She did not answer his smile. She had the feeling yet again that he wanted to be rid of her. His acceptance of her suggestion that he should lie down had been taken too docilely. There was nothing docile about John, nor was he in the habit of accepting advice.

'See you later then.' She had attempted to make her tone cool-sounding and offhand.

'Yes, see you later, Bridget.'

She had the desire to bang the door behind her and it was with an effort that she closed it quietly. As she hesitated for a moment, she saw Nancy coming from the direction of her grandmother's door and making her way to the back staircase. The old servant smiled towards her and paused in her walk. Bridget, glancing swiftly about her, went hastily forward, for it was apparent that Nancy wanted to speak to her.

'Grandmother's lying down, Nancy.'

'Yes, Miss Bridget. Miss Frances just told me. I just wanted to see if she'd be fancying anything special for her tea, she hardly touched her lunch . . . And you, Miss Bridget?' Nancy was whispering now. 'How are you? How's your arm?'

'Oh, much better, Nancy, thanks. It's only being a nuisance now.'

'Can . . . Can I say, Miss Bridget, how sorry I am for the trouble that's on you.' She put her hand out tentatively and touched Bridget's hand. 'But it'll all come right in the end. I have a feeling; it's the Irish in me.' She smiled. 'One that tells me you'll find a new life away from here.' Her voice grew lower. 'You're too fine china for a rough kitchen, if you'll forgive the expression, miss. Now I'll have Kate bring you up a tasty tray when she brings up madam's. There's nothing like getting something inside of you to bring a bit of comfort.'

'Thanks, Nancy, but I wouldn't bother, not about me, so long as you see to Grandma.'

'Oh, I'll see to something for you. I can always wangle a tea, but not a dinner, that being sent from the dining-room, as you know. Now I must away, and good luck to you, Miss Bridget, if I shouldn't be seeing you again.'

'Thanks, Nancy, thanks.' She smiled gratefully at the old woman, then said, 'I'm going down to the study, which is why I came this way.'

'Oh, Miss . . .' Nancy put her finger to her lip. 'The mistress is in there. She ordered tea to be taken in at four o'clock.'

Bridget and Nancy looked at each other in silence; then Bridget said, 'All right, Nancy, thanks for telling me, and . . . and I'll be seeing you before I go.'

'Oh, that'll be nice, miss. Bye-bye, miss.'

'Bye-bye, Nancy.' Bridget turned slowly away and walked to her room.

The study had always been acknowledged as Hester Gether's room when she was visiting Balderstone. It was to this room that she invited her friends from the surrounding neighbourhood to tea. It was in this room that Frances and she sat most of the time. The study was . . . Grandma's room. In ordering her tea to be served there today, Sarah Overmeer had emphasised not only the fact that she was mistress of this house, but any influence that Hester Gether had had on it, or any consideration she had received from its owner, was at an end.

The sadness in Bridget deepened. When she entered her room again she went straight to the chair by the rain-streaked window. Sitting down, she turned her head into the corner of it and slowly and painfully she began to cry.

Bridget was pacing the floor when she heard the first bell ring for dinner. It seemed distant tonight, muffled by the wind, and she stopped and smiled sadly to herself at its sound. It would, she thought, take nothing less than murder to prevent Aunt Sarah being formal. She was to remember this thought within a very short time and shudder at it. But she wondered now who would go into dinner; definitely Aunt Sarah and Uncle Vance, if he were in. And she guessed Laurence would dine too, for Laurence liked his food. But she doubted whether Grandma would join them. As for John, she felt sure he wouldn't either. She also wondered if Aunt Sarah would forbid Kate bringing her meal upstairs. She wouldn't be surprised, in which case she would go hungry, for under no circumstances could she go to the dining-room.

For the past hour or more she had waited for someone to come in: her grandmother, or Frances . . . or John, but no-one had come near her; nor had she heard any sound outside her room, except that of the storm. Silence weighed the house down and she had the feeling of being a prisoner within a stone fortress. But she comforted herself, telling herself it was only a matter of hours until tomorrow.

She was standing at the window when the second bell rang. The rain had eased a little. It was thinner, the drops discernible and not at such an acute angle. She could see over the garden, and in the far far distance the hazy outline of Mickle Fell. In strong contrast to the inside of the house the outside world was all movement, the trees swaying and bending, the thick, solid yew hedges shivering under the impact of the wind. The very garden ornaments seemed to be leaning back to resist being toppled over. With all this movement why were her eyes brought down to a grey blur at the far end of the drive where it curved away from the house? Perhaps because of it everything else in sight seemed stationary. When it did move it was stiff and straight and it kept close to the hedge that bordered the drive, until it came nearer to the house.

Bridget's face was close to the window now, her eyes screwed up as she peered out, and when she recognised the moving blur – more by its height and shape than what she could make out of its features – her breath, exhaling after a long gasp, blurred the pane and by the time her hand had wiped it clean again, the figure had vanished.

Had she imagined it? No. That figure would be imprinted for ever on her mind. The woman down there was Mrs Crofton. But why was she coming to the house? She must be mad. But mad wasn't the right word. Bridget felt slightly sick as Bruce's words came back to her once again: loving like savages.

She was on the point of turning from the window when her attention was caught again by a movement to the left of her. Someone – a man – was coming from the side of the house. It should have been Laurence, but it wasn't; it was John who was moving towards the drive. He was enveloped in a raincoat, the collar up, a cap pulled well down over his eyes.

She watched him enter the drive, his stride characteristically quick, and then she became puzzled when she saw him slacken his pace to a slow walk. She was puzzled further when he stopped once and looked about him. Then with startling suddenness his actions were explained: from out of the hedge stepped the grey figure of Mrs Crofton. For a moment Bridget watched them. They seemed to be talking; then together they disappeared through one of the archways that led from the drive into the garden and were lost to her sight.

She moved from the window and looked

dazedly around the room. John meeting Mrs Crofton? And by appointment? That was no chance meeting. He had known she was there . . . John meeting Mrs Crofton? There was a sudden sharp stab between her ribs and she shook her head as she said to herself, Don't be silly, she couldn't want John too . . . No, but John might want her. What did she know of John, really? He had known Mrs Crofton a long time, even before Laurence had come on the scene. Was that why he married so quickly, a loveless marriage, made out of compassion? You didn't do a thing like that unless you were hurt in some way, unless you felt there wasn't much left in life. She hadn't thought of it like that before, but now she was thinking, and thinking hard. She remembered that John had never said a word against Mrs Crofton. He had even said, 'Don't think too badly of her.' Thinking back, she remembered him speak of Mrs Crofton. It was a long time ago. His words had been, She is a fascinating woman.

'Oh, that woman! That woman!' Bridget found herself speaking aloud. And John? What was he thinking about to meet her in the grounds almost under Laurence's nose, and after what happened this afternoon? But perhaps the meeting had been arranged before that. The thought brought a feeling of anger spurting up in her. She felt she was being betrayed for the second time in a few days. She hated Mrs Crofton . . . Oh, she hated her!

When the clock on the mantelpiece struck the half-hour Bridget went swiftly from the room. Her emotions had moved now to indignation and this was directed towards Sarah Overmeer. It was as she had surmised: she was to have no meal sent upstairs.

How petty, how utterly petty! She would go and see what Grandma had to say about it. Likely she was to starve, too.

When she knocked on her grandmother's door there was no response, and on opening it she found the room empty. This did not lessen her indignation. So Grandma *had* gone down after all. But why hadn't she called in to see her first?

She returned to the landing but did not go to her room. She would go downstairs and into the study. She would have to go to the room anyway before tomorrow, because she had left a number of letters in the writing-table drawer. And should she come across Kate she would say to her, 'Be kind enough to bring my dinner up to my room.' And on this she almost marched down the stairs.

The wall lights were on in the hall, and although the wind was roaring around the house she could hear muffled sounds from behind the closed doors of the dining-room, which told her that MacKay was busy with the dishes at the sideboard; whereupon the saliva began to run in her mouth.

Before she entered the study she went into the cloakroom that was near the front door and from the pegs she lifted two coats, one a light-weight mackintosh, the other a scarlet leather jerkin. She would pack these in her trunk: it would save carrying them tomorrow.

She had the coats across her arm as she went into the study. The room was almost dark, and the wind here, hitting the front of the house full blast, was deafening. The French windows were rattling and the noise in the wide chimney was like that of a train in a tunnel.

Dropping the coats onto a chair that stood between the writing-table and the French window she pulled open the long top drawer of the table and took out her letters. Bunching them together she closed the drawer and was bending forward to pick up her coats when with the swiftness of lightning the French windows burst open and she was almost knocked off her feet. She leant back against the wall, waiting for the entry of whoever had thrust open the doors, and it was a full minute before she realised there was no-one there waiting to pounce on her, and that the French windows had been blown open with the force of the gale. The room was alive with the elements.

With her good arm she tried to pull one half of the window closed, while the rain soaked her and the wind threatened to lift her from her feet. Not being able to pull the window forward she went behind it and, putting her good shoulder to it, gradually pushed it into place.

She was struggling with the other half of the window when the door opened and Kate entered the room. She stood for a moment gaping, then exclaimed in astonishment, 'Oh, miss! Whatever are you doing?'

It seemed obvious what Bridget was doing and even if she had had breath with which to reply she saw no need to answer. But after Kate had applied her robust strength to the windows and they were securely locked top and bottom, Bridget lay back against the glass for a moment and closed her eyes, both in fatigue and against Kate, who was saying, 'Whatever have you been up to, miss?'

Bridget wiped the rain from her face with her hand and stroked back her wet hair, then picked up the letters and coats from the chair.

'You'll get your death being out in that, miss,

and you just over a shock.' There was a reprimanding tone in Kate's voice.

'I haven't been out; the windows blew open.'

'But you're wringing wet, miss.'

'Yes, yes, I know that, but I couldn't get them closed.'

Kate, her mouth slightly agape, stared at Bridget, then said, 'I took your dinner up, miss, and you weren't in. You shouldn't 'ave gone out.'

Oh, what was the use! She saw no point in explaining further.

She went past Kate and across the hall and up to her room once again, the room that she was beginning to loathe. There was the tray set out appetisingly, but now she seemed to have lost the desire for food. She was picking over the meal when her grandmother at last came into the room.

The old lady looked rather sad as she sat down and asked, 'Did you think I was lost?'

'I haven't known what to think. I haven't seen anyone but Kate for hours.'

'And feeling a little sorry for yourself?'

'Yes, a little, Grandma.' Bridget was forced to smile. 'Where have you been? I went to your room.'

'Well, I went downstairs before dinner to say

a personal goodbye to Nancy. I have always liked Nancy; she is a good woman, as MacKay is a good man. I wish I could say the same of Kate and that outside man, Ryder. One is a frustrated spinster if ever I've met one, and the man a sensation-monger. That man has always wanted to ingratiate himself into people's good books. Anyway, as I said, I wanted to say goodbye to Nancy, and as she knew I wasn't going down to dinner she was kind enough to make me up something which I ate in her room, and later she came in and we sat talking; because I knew, and she knew, that after tomorrow we wouldn't meet again.'

Bridget bowed her head at this and said softly, 'It's as Aunt Sarah says, I feel I am to blame for all this.'

'Nonsense. Now stop that, Bridget. There's one person to blame and that's Laurence, and you know it, and I know it, and everybody in this house knows it. But perhaps the Crofton woman should take some share of the blame in this case . . . By the way, where's John?'

It seemed odd that her Grandma had mentioned John in the same breath with Mrs Crofton's name. Perhaps it was only coincidence. 'I saw him going out just before dinner.'

'Just before dinner? It was pelting heavens hard then. Where was he off to?'

'I don't know, Grandma. He didn't look in.'

'Well, that was a stupid thing to do. And he should be the first person to know it. To go out in drenching rain like that! What on earth was he thinking about? You have no idea where he's gone?'

'No, Grandma. Perhaps . . .' Bridget paused, 'not wanting to go down to dinner he might have gone to the Stag.' She did not look at the old lady as she spoke.

'Well, I should have thought he would have preferred an empty stomach to a drenching. Anyway, he could have gone in to Nancy. She would have seen to him: he knows that.'

'May I come in?' This request was accompanied by a tapping on the door and caused Bridget and her grandmother to exchange quick glances. It was the old lady who called, 'Yes, come in,' and it was she who demanded, 'Where have you been?'

John, now dressed in grey slacks and a thick wool sweater, repeated, 'Where have I been? What do you mean, Grandma?'

'Just what I say: what possessed you to go out in this?'

'Oh!' He paused and jerked his head back as

if nonplussed by the question. 'Oh! I just wanted some fresh air, bracing air; I was being stifled in here.'

'You didn't go out for a meal?'

'A meal?' He brought his head down to hers.

'Yes, you've had no dinner, have you?'

'No, I haven't, Grandma. And what is more, I don't feel hungry.'

'Nonsense! You haven't had a bite since lunch. Go down to Nancy and she'll get you something. You need fortifying in all ways after that business this afternoon.'

'Oh, I couldn't, Grandma, not at this time. Look,' – he showed her his watch – 'it's turned eight-thirty; she'll be cleared away.'

'You go down to Nancy and get something to eat. Go down by the back stairs so you won't run into anyone.'

For answer, John turned and, smiling faintly at Bridget, asked, 'What can you do with her? Isn't she a dominant old fishwife?' It was evident he was trying hard to be his old self.

Bridget found herself staring unsmiling at John. When she didn't answer him he came to her side, and sitting down beside her asked, 'How do you feel?'

'All right.'

'What's the matter?'

'Nothing.'

He screwed up his eyes at her. Then turning to the old lady, he asked, 'Anything happened since I last saw you, Grandma?'

'What makes you ask that? Nothing further has happened to my knowledge . . . you . . . you don't know of anything do you, Bridget?' The old lady was also peering at Bridget now, and she, facing her grandmother in preference to looking at John, replied, 'Nothing that I know of.'

Whatever reasons John had for meeting Mrs Crofton he wanted to hide them, and whatever she felt personally about his underhand conduct she couldn't give him away.

'What prompted you to ask her if anything had happened?' The old lady had turned her narrowed eyes on John who, smiling quietly, replied, 'Just my sense of diagnosis.'

'Your sense of . . . ?'

The old lady's voice was cut off by a quick discreet tapping on the door, and it was she again who called, 'Come in.'

It was MacKay who entered, saying, 'Excuse me, madam, but there's a call for the doctor.'

John had risen to his feet. 'Where from?' he asked, 'London?'

'They didn't say long distance, sir. It's a

gentleman, but he wouldn't give his name.'

When John followed MacKay from the room, the old lady, looking hard at Bridget again, said, 'He thinks something happened and we're keeping it from him.' Her thin neck stretched forward now from out of her dress. 'He was quizzing you. Nothing *has* happened, Bridget . . . Look at me.'

'I'm looking at you, Grandma.'

'Has anything happened?'

'No. No, of course not.'

'You were stiff with John, now I come to think of it, and he noticed it.'

'I'm not feeling very fit or playful at the moment, Grandma.'

The old lady bent forward now, catching Bridget's hand and patting it. 'I know, my dear, I know. This business has been simply awful for you and you have behaved remarkably well, remarkably well, and you won't have to put up with it much longer. A good night's rest and then tomorrow we'll be off. I'm going to bed now myself. I'll just wait until John comes back and then I'll away to my room. And I'm going to tell you something. You won't believe it, but it's true. Very soon you'll have put this all behind you . . . It'll hardly be a memory.'

'I'd like to believe you, Grandma.'

'And why not? Because what I tell you is true. You'll look upon this as a lucky escape, my dear.'

'Grandma.' Bridget shook her head as she murmured, 'Don't forget I was to be married shortly.'

'I don't forget, Bridget, dear . . . But sh!' She lifted up her finger. 'Here's John.'

The door was opened, but only slightly, and John stood there, saying, 'May I see you for a moment, Grandma?'

With her eyebrows slightly raised Hester Gether rose stiffly to her feet and went out of the room, pulling the door behind her. And Bridget waited. What was the matter? John looked awful, white and stricken. Then the sound of anguish in her grandmother's voice, exclaiming, 'Oh no! Oh no!' brought Bridget to the door.

'What must I do?' Again her grandmother's voice. And then John's tense whisper, 'Do nothing yet. Go in with her. Stay there until I get back. Dickenson's at the phone box on the main road.'

As the door was pushed slowly open Bridget asked, 'What is it, Grandma? What is it? Oh, be careful! You'll fall. Come and sit down.' She put her arm round the old lady and helped her faltering steps towards a chair. 'What's happened? What did John say? I heard him mention Dickenson. Oh, what's happened, Grandma? Tell me.'

'Wait a minute, child, wait a minute. Look.' The old lady closed her eyes. 'Ring for Frances. No . . . no, don't do that, she gets excited . . . Get me a glass of water.'

Bridget rushed to the bathroom, and returning with a glass of water, held it to her grandmother's lips. The wrinkled skin looked like parchment now. Her mouth was loose and her lower lip trembling, as were her hands.

'Something dreadful has happened, hasn't it?' Bridget was crouching over the old lady and Hester Gether, her eyes full of what Bridget would not countenance as fear, whispered, 'Yes, something dreadful has happened.' She caught hold of Bridget's hand as she gasped out, 'Laurence is lying outside the cedar hut: he has been shot. Bruce Dickenson told John on the phone that . . . that he's dead.'

Bridget felt her whole body sagging. She began to shake her head from side to side. No, not that! Oh, not that! Her mind was gabbling now. I wouldn't wish him dead. Oh no . . .! And Aunt Sarah? Oh, Aunt Sarah! She said in a thin whisper, 'Aunt Sarah.'

'Yes . . . Aunt Sarah. Sarah . . . Poor Sarah.'

'But who? Who would do it? . . . Bruce? Oh, no! No!'

'I can't tell you anything further, Bridget. I can only tell you what John said. We must sit here and wait. Get me another glass of water, please.'

They sat without speaking for at least twenty minutes. The old lady did not move from her chair but Bridget felt compelled, every now and again, to walk about the room; it was as much as she could do not to dash downstairs. Whenever any sound came from the landing, or the hall, she would stop and strain her ears, and her grandmother, head to one side, would also listen.

But when the terrible news burst on the house there was no need to strain their ears to hear, for Sarah's voice came loud and shrill, crying, 'Leave me alone! I must see him.' Then someone cried, 'Oh, my God! My God!' This, Bridget knew, was Frances, and the words were uttered in swift repetition as she approached the bedroom door and unceremoniously thrust it open. And she stood clutching the front of her dress. Then, meeting the waiting eyes of her mistress, she tried to regain some control over her emotions, as she whispered, 'Oh, madam, madam, something dreadful has happened. Dreadful, dreadful.'

'Close the door, Frances. We know, Frances, we know.'

'You do, madam? But they've only—'

'Yes, yes, but the doctor told us some time ago.'

'Mrs Overmeer's in a dreadful state.'

'I'll come down . . . You stay here, Bridget.'

'No, Grandma, I'm coming with you.'

The old lady did not argue and Bridget followed her out of the room and across the landing, and when they were at the head of the stairs she took hold of her grandmother's arm to steady her descent. The hall seemed crowded with people, all men. There was Ryder and MacKay and John and her Uncle Vance, but there was no sign of Laurence, or Sarah Overmeer, but the eyes of the men looking in the direction of the study explained where the mother and son were.

The old lady, moving slowly towards Vance, came to a stop by his side, and as she directed her gaze towards the study she said, 'Oh! Vance, Vance, this is dreadful, shocking.'

Bridget dragged her eyes from the study door to her uncle's face to find that the suave plausible man of the world was gone. She was looking at an old man, who seemed to be momentarily deranged, for he looked dull, even stupid. There was something so pathetic about him that she was forced to move towards him and was in the act of doing so when an almost unperceivable shake of John's head bade her stay where she was.

They all stood waiting silently, staring at the door for what appeared to Bridget to be an endless length of time, until her grandmother said quietly, 'Don't you think you had better go in, Vance?'

For answer she received a slow shake from his head, and it was at this point that the door opened and Sarah Overmeer entered the hall.

Her aunt, too, looked changed, but not in the same way as her uncle. There was no sign of tears on her deathly white face. She was not stooped or dazed with grief; her body if anything seemed straighter. She just stood there, looking like some dark angel guarding the tomb of her dead. Her eyes now slowly travelled from one face to another, to come to rest on Bridget's, and it was to Bridget she spoke, each word seeming to be encased in ice, so cold was her voice, so colourless her tone. 'You have done this to me,' she said.

'No! No, Aunt Sarah!' Bridget's voice was a faint protesting squeak coming from high up in her head, and she groped for protection to the hand that was nearest to her and found it clasped in that of John's. And again she protested, 'Oh, no, Aunt Sarah.'

'Oh, yes, Bridget Gether. Your farmer friend took up the cudgels for you and my son is dead.'

John, relinquishing Bridget's hand, moved towards the stiff terrible figure in the doorway, saying gently, 'Aunt Sarah, Bruce Dickenson didn't do this thing.'

'Who then? You? Did you decide to finish off what you failed to do this afternoon?'

John paused within two feet of the woman whom he remembered had at times been very kind to him, and he bowed his head; but he raised it sharply as Sarah's voice, addressing MacKay, said, 'You have sent for the doctor and the police?'

Before MacKay could answer John put in quietly, 'They're on their way.' His face full of pity as he looked at the distraught woman, he added, 'Bruce Dickenson phoned for them when he phoned me. They should be here at any moment.'

Sarah looked at John, but before she spoke again she lifted the full force of her fearful glance to Bridget, and, her words dripping bitterness, she said, 'That was clever of your friend, but it won't help him, for I'll see that he pays for tonight's work.'

Seven

'John, if they ask me the same thing again I'll go mad, I just can't stand it.'

'Well, they will ask you again . . . and again, and you'll stand it because you are speaking the truth.'

'But they believe Kate.'

'You don't know who those fellows believe. I know they don't believe me, and they don't believe Bruce.'

'Poor Bruce! You know, I feel sorry for Bruce. I suppose in a way I should hate him, because all this really did start through him, but I can't. I can only feel sorry for him.'

'It didn't start with Bruce, Bridget. A thing like this has its beginnings far back, and you know it.'

Yes, yes, she knew it; she knew that if

Laurence hadn't played a double game, he would have been alive now.

She looked up at John's tense grey face. He seemed to have put on ten years in the past few days. She said dully, 'Why do they want us all again this morning?'

'Your guess is as good as mine.' He glanced at his watch. 'I think we had better be getting downstairs.' Rising to his feet, he held out his hand and she took it and they stood looking at each other until Bridget whispered, 'Oh, John, I'm so frightened.'

'You've nothing to be afraid of.' He touched her cheek. 'If our consciences were all as clear as yours, we would have nothing to fear.'

She was staring into his deep, soft brown eyes as she thought, He means *his* conscience. At the three inquiries that had gone before he had made no mention of his meeting with Mrs Crofton on the night Laurence was killed. In fact, her name had not come up at all. He had maintained firmly that he had gone for a walk in the direction of the village between seven and eight on that evening and to prove it he had called as witnesses a Mr and Mrs Pinder, who lived in a cottage on the road to the village. Moreover, he said he had directed a car driver to West Auckland. He remembered that the car was a

Rover and the driver of it had a Vandyke beard. His statement had been proved true when the driver of the car was contacted in Auckland, but still he had made no mention of Mrs Crofton.

Again she asked herself if Mrs Crofton had been in John's life before Bruce had entered hers?

These last few days, since she had emerged from her cocoon, she had been forced to look at life, and she didn't like what she saw. She wished, oh, she wished she could go back to the time when everyone had appeared nice, when she refused to think badly of anyone, when there was the simple pleasure of painting and the glorious feeling of being in love. But being in love the way she had been she now knew was but a mirage born of adolescent desire.

'Come, don't look so sad. It will soon be over, and as I've said, you've got nothing to fear.' He stroked her cheek with the back of his knuckles as he had often done when she was a child, and she found the action hurt her. She moved away from him saying, 'I can't help being afraid of Kate.'

'Well, you mustn't let her see it. Kate's in the limelight and she's making the best of it. But these policemen aren't fools; they know how these things are exaggerated. Come, we'd better go now.' He put his arm around her shoulders and pressed her gently to him for a moment, and she did not resist the comfort of his embrace. Then he led her from the room and down the stairs, and into the drawing-room.

They all sat in the same positions as they had done during the three previous inquiries; all in a semicircle facing the small table, behind which sat the inspector, and at his side a plain-clothes man, who occupied himself with making notes for most of the time. Bridget and John sat centrally in the semicircle on the deep couch. To Bridget's right sat Kate, Ryder and MacKay. To John's left, sitting stiffly upright in a straight-backed chair, sat Hester Gether, and at the extremity of the semicircle, and seemingly quite apart, was Bruce Dickenson.

Bruce Dickenson looked haggard. He looked like a man who was ill and suffering mentally, but his voice was steady when he answered the inspector, saying, 'It's as I have already told you, sir.'

'Yes. Hmm!' The inspector was a thick-set man who looked as if he was associated more with farming than with the police force. He had a pleasant, even jovial countenance, and there was no evidence in his expression that behind it lay a probing mind. He looked down at a sheaf of papers on the table and again said, 'Hmm!' then added, as if reading from the paper, 'You say, Mr Dickenson, that you received a letter late on the afternoon of the seventeenth of September purporting to come from Miss Bridget Gether?' His eyebrows flicked upwards and his eyes moved in Bridget's direction before he proceeded, 'You say it was delivered to you by a boy. When you asked the boy who had sent it he told you it was given to him by a Mr MacKay, but when the boy is confronted by MacKay he says he isn't the man who gave him the letter . . . yet you received the letter, Mr Dickenson . . . right?'

'Yes, sir.'

'And you proceeded to do as it requested . . . you went to what is known as . . . the pond in the grounds of this house?'

'Yes, sir.'

'You expected to see Miss Gether there?'

'Yes, sir.'

'But you saw lying by the side of the cedar hut the body of Mr Laurence Overmeer?'

'Yes, sir.'

'You saw that he had been shot through the chest. You also saw a gun lying by his side. You touched neither the gun nor him but hurried away, because you were afraid someone would come and you would get the blame. Is that correct, Mr Dickenson?'

'Yes, sir, that is what I've said.'

'Well, we know now that the boy recognised from a photograph the man who gave him the note to hand to you. That man was Mr Laurence Overmeer. Now would you like to think again, Mr Dickenson. Perhaps . . . I am just putting it to you . . . that Mr Overmeer was not dead when you first saw him. You expected to see Miss Gether but you were confronted by the man she was at one time, and very recently, going to marry. You have admitted that you were interested in Miss Gether but received no encouragement. Is that—?'

'You are not in a court of law yet, sir; your touching on this personal matter is quite beside the point.'

The inspector was looking at the indignant old lady and his voice was quiet, even gentle, as he replied, 'Madam, there is nothing beside the point when you're trying to get at the truth. Mr Laurence Overmeer was not shot because someone was playing with a gun. He was killed because of a motive. I think we've established that much.'

'I maintain, sir, that your question is irrelevant, and Mr Dickenson, I would remind you, is not on trial for his life.'

'No, true, madam, not yet; there is no-one on trial for his life, as yet.'

There was movement in the room as Bruce Dickenson rose to his feet. His voice was unsteady now and the fingers of his hands were locked together as he said, 'I have told you the truth. I did not shoot Mr Overmeer. I found him dead and I went to the phone and rang Dr MacDonald.'

'Yes, yes, you did.' The inspector nodded his head. 'And now I would like to ask you why you particularly rang Dr MacDonald?'

Bruce Dickenson looked towards the couch, then again to the inspector as he replied, 'Because we used to talk together quite a bit years ago and . . . and we had talked that particular afternoon, as I've already told you. He had heard I wasn't well and was kind enough to call and see me. But the real reason why I rang him was because I knew him to be a level-headed gentleman.'

'Very well. Sit down, Mr Dickenson.'

As Bridget watched Bruce Dickenson lower himself into his chair with the action of an aged man, it was borne home to her that what John had said a few moments ago in the bedroom was true. The blame went far back. In this case to herself, for she was the real cause of Bruce Dickenson being in this predicament because of those summer nights when she had run from the house to meet him and had roamed the woods with him. If the blame was to be apportioned out correctly her share would be large.

'And now, Miss Gether.' The inspector's voice made her start and she looked straight at the man. He was smiling at her, even kindly, but that meant nothing for she knew he would cut her to shreds in the course of his duty and think nothing of it. 'And now, Miss Gether, you say here' – the inspector was holding a piece of paper delicately between his finger and thumb – 'that you never left the house on the evening of the seventeenth of September. Yet the maid, Miss Kate Brownlow' – he inclined his head towards where Kate was sitting prim and important – 'says she was drawn to the study by the sound of the French windows being thrust open, and when she entered the room she saw you coming from outside.'

'She did not see me entering the room, sir, for I had never been out of it.' These were the same words that Bridget had used on the three previous occasions. They sounded to her now as if she were reading them.

The inspector dropped his eyes to the paper in

his hand and looked at it quietly for some minutes before raising his glance to Bridget again. 'You say you came downstairs to get some letters from the bureau in the study and just as you were about to do this the wind burst open the French windows and you had great difficulty in closing them, and your clothes became wet with the rain.'

'That is correct.'

The inspector pursed his lips and drew in a long breath before stating, 'We have ascertained that it was a north-easterly gale blowing that night. The French windows of the study face west; even with a blustery wind it is hard to believe you were soaked to the skin as you have described.'

'I was very wet.'

'In the short time it would take you to close the window?'

'I could only use one arm, sir; as I have already told you, my shoulder was put out some time ago.' In the quietness that followed this statement Bridget was conscious of the movement of Bruce Dickenson's chair.

'Why, if you had only come downstairs to collect your letters did you have a mackintosh with you?'

Bridget began to shiver. She half-turned her

head in John's direction; then looking at the inspector again, she said, 'As I have already told you a number of times, I went into the cloakroom and took a mackintosh and a jerkin that were hanging there. I took them to pack so I wouldn't have to carry them the following day when I intended to leave.'

'Yes, yes, you have told us all this before, Miss Gether. I am sorry that you have to repeat yourself but it is necessary. Now' – he again consulted the paper – 'according to the evidence given by Miss Kate Brownlow, she overheard you telling Mr Overmeer that you felt like killing him.'

Bridget closed her eyes and gulped audibly before she brought out, 'Yes, yes, I have told you that it is quite true, but as I said, it was during a quarrel.'

'Why did you feel so strongly against the man you were planning to marry?'

'I was not going to marry him when I said that: the marriage had been broken off.'

'Yes, yes, I understand that, but what forced you to make such a strong statement? What had he done to you that made you want to kill him? You have not as yet given us an answer to this question.'

Bridget bowed her head, and when there came

an exclamation of protest from both John and Hester Gether, the inspector said, 'Very well, very well,' and then added curtly, 'I am not doing this for pleasure.'

'You surprise me!' At this rejoinder from the formidable old lady the inspector took refuge in his notes once more. And now he was addressing John.

'And you, Dr MacDonald. In the afternoon on the day in question, did you attempt to kill Mr Overmeer?'

'I did not.'

'Will you explain again what happened?'

John's mouth opened and closed once more before he began tersely, 'Mr Overmeer was annoying Miss Gether—'

'Annoying Miss Gether? The young lady he was going to marry . . . annoying her?'

'I said annoying her, and I meant annoying her. I told him to leave her alone. When he wouldn't I struck at him and then he came for me.'

'And you lifted a heavy bronze urn and levelled it at his head?'

'Mr Overmeer was the worse for drink; he was a very powerful man and I was in no condition to combat him. I grabbed at the first thing that came to hand.'

'It was a very murderous object, Dr MacDonald. If the point of the urn had pierced his head as it did the picture on the wall he might have died earlier than he did. You, as a doctor, would admit that?'

'I admit no such thing.'

The inspector sighed as if he were sorry for many things. 'Now then, Dr MacDonald, we move to later that day. You have stated that between the hours of seven and eight you went for a walk.'

'That is so.'

'You went for a walk during one of the worst storms we have had this year.'

'Yes.'

'But haven't you said that the reason you were in no condition to combat Mr Overmeer when he was about to attack you was because of a recent illness?'

'That is so.'

'Then you, being a doctor and knowing that it would not help your present condition to become wet through, go out into a storm just because you felt like a walk?'

'Yes . . . just because I felt like a walk.'

'I would suggest that you are not telling the truth, Dr MacDonald.'

Bridget felt the tremor that passed through

John's body and she couldn't look at him, or the inspector when he went on, and now briskly, 'You went out that night, Dr MacDonald, to meet someone. You had an appointment to meet someone. Is that not so?'

There was no reply to this. 'Come now, Doctor, it would help this inquiry if you would tell us whom you went to meet, and why.'

There was still no reply, and the inspector, after jerking his head with a movement that said plainly, Well I've done my best for you, turned to where Ryder was sitting and said, 'Will you, Mr Ryder, tell us what you saw on the night in question?'

Ryder moved on his chair, and keeping his eyes fixed on the inspector, he began in stilted tones, 'I was walking across the courtyard from the stables when I happened to look up and see the doctor standing at the window. He was behaving funnily and I stopped.'

'What do you mean by .. behaving funnily?'

'Well, sir, he was pointing to himself.'

'Describe what you mean.'

All the eyes in the room were now turned to where Ryder was digging at his chest with his finger.

'The action was as if he was looking at someone and saying "Me?"'

'Yes, sir, that could be it.'

'He wasn't looking at you?'

'No, sir, I was to the side of him, and he must have been looking over the coachhouse on to the drive.'

'But could he see anyone on the drive; wasn't it raining heavily?'

'Not at that moment, sir. It was raining but not all that much; he could have seen on the drive.'

'What did you do next?'

'Well, sir, I went into the stables and picked up my cycling cape, because I knew that I would need it for going to and fro, because we were in for a long storm.'

'And then what happened?'

'Well, I made my way then to the back door, and when I was going into the passage that leads to the back staircase and the kitchen Dr MacDonald came hurrying out.'

'Did he speak to you?'

'No. He just pushed past me.'

'What was his manner like? Calm? Flustered? Angry? Distraught?'

'Well, sir, not angry, and not calm, either; a bit flustered, I should say.'

'What did you do then?'

'Well, sir, I was interested to know who he had

been signalling to on the drive, and so . . . well, sir, I followed him at a discreet distance.'

'And what did you see?'

'Well, it was raining more heavy now, sir, but just as I got round the curve of the drive I saw him going under the arch into the garden.'

'Was he alone?'

'No, sir, there was a lady with him.'

'Do you know who that lady was?'

'I . . . I can't rightly say, sir; it was raining, as I said.'

'But do you think you know who that lady was?'

Ryder's eyes dropped away from the inspector's, but the inspector's voice, crisp now, was saying, 'Come along, repeat what you told me earlier. You think you know who that lady was. Tell me her name.'

'I think it was Miss Bridget, sir.'

'No! No!' Bridget's half-choked denial was checked by John's hand gripping her arm. 'But, John.' Bridget was now staring into John's face and he was saying, 'It's all right, Bridget.'

'What have you to say to this, Doctor?'

John jerked his head round towards the inspector and rapped out, 'I say, Inspector, that you are barking up the wrong tree. Ryder is correct in this case; I did meet a lady, although it wasn't Miss Gether, and if his eyes were as sharp as they usually are he would have seen that.'

'What was the marked difference, Doctor, that Mr Ryder should have detected?'

'I'll leave that for you to find out, sir . . . And may I enquire . . .?' John turned his angry countenance towards where Ryder was standing with his head bowed, 'And may I enquire why Ryder has not exposed my deception earlier?'

'He thought it would come out in the course of events, didn't you, Mr Ryder?'

The inspector looked towards the man but received no answer, then went on, 'But when it didn't he thought it might help clear up this very muddled affair. Now, would you like to take us a step further, Doctor, and tell us the name of the lady you met?'

'No, I wouldn't.'

'Perhaps you've got a very strong reason for not wishing her name to be mentioned?'

'I have not said that. I . . . I just don't see any reason why she should be involved.'

'No? Even if it meant suspicion falling on Miss Gether?'

'No suspicion would fall on Miss Gether through any action of mine. I can only state plainly that it wasn't Miss Gether I met that night.'

'Well, Doctor,' – the inspector pushed his hands through his sparse hair – 'if you won't give us any help along this particular route there is nothing left to me but to jog your memory.' The inspector turned at this point and nodded towards his companion, who seemed to be waiting for such a sign, for immediately he rose to his feet and went out of the room, leaving the company alerted, their eyes directed towards the dining-room door. That is, all except John, who now, with his hands pressed between his knees, gazed in the direction of his feet.

Bridget turned and looked at her grandmother, but the old lady just shook her head slightly. Her grandmother didn't know who they were going to bring into the room but she, Bridget, did. She dropped her head now down to the level of John's and whispered, 'I'm sorry, John, I'm sorry.'

Her tone brought his eyes glancing sideways at her, but there was no time for more because the drawing-room door now opened and there, preceding the young policeman into the room, appeared Joyce Crofton. John was on his feet, as was Bruce Dickenson and MacKay: only the inspector and Ryder remained seated.

Bridget watched the young policeman pull forward a chair. She watched Mrs Crofton sit down. She found she could not take her eyes off this woman who had played such a painful part in her life, yet now, as on the last time she had met her, she found it impossible to hate her. She had been sorry for her on the other occasion, but not now. Yet the man she had loved, whom they had both loved, was dead. Had she murdered Laurence? It was not the first time that this thought had presented itself to Bridget's mind, and she had wanted to voice it, but the only one she could really talk to objectively about the matter was John and he had made it impossible by his silence on the very vital point of why he had gone out for a walk in the rain. She watched him now staring across the room at the deathly pale, beautiful woman.

Mrs Crofton was looking at no-one: she had her eyes fixed on some point above the inspector's head. And the inspector was now concentrating his gaze once again upon John.

'Is your memory any clearer now, Doctor?' The tone was slightly sarcastic.

John made no reply and the inspector slowly turned his gaze back to Mrs Crofton and said quietly, 'You are Mrs Joyce Crofton of The Hillocks, Mickle Taggart?'

Joyce Crofton inclined her head just the slightest. 'And you were a friend of the deceased man, Mr Laurence Overmeer?'

Again there was a slow movement of the head.

'A close friend?'

Mrs Crofton remained motionless now and there was silence in the room for a moment, apart from the sharp censorious cough which came from Hester Gether. Whether it was directed against the inspector or the woman under question was not quite clear.

'In a statement you made last evening you said that you came into the grounds of Balderstone about quarter to seven on the evening of September the seventeenth. Is that correct, Mrs Crofton?'

'That is correct.' The voice was low yet clear.

'Did you come into the grounds for any particular purpose?'

'Yes.'

'What was that purpose?'

'I . . . I wanted help.'

'Why didn't you come boldly to the house?'

'Because' – the eyes were cast down – 'because my presence would not have been welcome.'

'For whom were you seeking help?'

'For Mr Dickenson.' Her voice was a mere whisper now, but it sharpened everyone's attention and it brought Bruce Dickenson's body upright as he actually gaped at the lowered head of this undoubtedly attractive woman.

'Will you go on to explain, Mrs Crofton, why you thought Mr Dickenson required help.'

The long full throat swelled, then contracted as Mrs Crofton swallowed before she began to speak. 'Mr Laurence Overmeer phoned me around six o'clock. I realised he . . . he had been drinking. He was talking very wildly about Mr Dickenson and . . . Miss Gether. He said Mr Dickenson badly wanted to meet Miss Gether and he was arranging an appointment for him that evening. At first I thought it was just wild talk, then something he said made me realise that he was going to . . .' She stopped and lowered her head, and the inspector put in quietly, 'He was going to shoot Mr Dickenson?'

'No! No, there was no mention of shooting. I only got the impression that he was going to . . . to fight him.'

The inspector cast his eyes down to the sheaf of papers on the table, and lifting the topmost one now, he perused it for a moment before saying, 'That wasn't exactly the term you used last night.'

'I was distraught last night.'

The inspector, ignoring this explanation, appeared to read from the paper. ' "He became very excited and said he would . . . pulp him up

... and then he rang off and I became very worried, so worried that I phoned Mr Dickenson. And when I was told he had gone out I got into my car and drove to Balderstone."

'Is that correct, Mrs Crofton?'

At this point Bridget wanted to cry out, Leave her alone! Leave her alone! The sight of this woman's suffering was almost unbearable to her. This woman had loved Laurence, not as she herself had loved him from behind the colourful screen of romance, but in a mad passionate way. And now he was dead and whether she had killed him or not she would always feel responsible for his death, for it was because of the intrigue between them that this had come about.

'So you came to Balderstone hoping to prevent Mr Overmeer doing Mr Dickenson a mischief?'

'Yes.'

'How did you propose to go about this?'

'I hoped to see one of the men, perhaps ... Mr Ryder, and ask him to go to the pool to see if Mr Overmeer was there.'

'You knew then the meeting place was to be at the pool?'

'Yes.'

'How did you come by this information?'

'By something Mr Overmeer had told me

earlier ... And ... and while on the phone he remarked that the pool had a specific attraction for Mr Dickenson.'

Bruce Dickenson's fingers nipped his mouth into a thin painful line as he stared fixedly at Mrs Crofton.

'And you didn't see Mr Ryder, Mrs Crofton?'

'No, it was raining: there was nobody about. But I happened to look at the windows above the stables and I saw Dr MacDonald standing there.'

'Well, go on. What did you do?'

'I signalled to him to come out, and he did.'

'Yes. What followed next?'

'I told him briefly what I feared, and together we went to the pool.'

'And what did you find there?'

'Nothing. There was no-one about and the hut was empty.'

'Did you look inside the hut?'

'No, the door was locked.'

'Did you wait to see what would transpire?'

'We waited for about fifteen minutes, then the storm became so fierce that Dr MacDonald took me back to my car.'

'And what did he say to you?'

'He said I was not to worry and he would keep a lookout.'

'And you left the matter in his hands?'

'Yes.'

'Don't you think that was rather odd after your concern for Mr Dickenson?'

Mrs Crofton was looking at her tightly clasped hands now. 'I . . . I was very wet . . . and slightly . . . distressed.'

'I did not quite catch that last word . . . was it distressed?'

Bridget, like her grandmother, felt an anger rising in her against the inspector's methods. Mrs Crofton's voice had been low but still clear. He knew the word was distressed, what was he trying to do? Make her break down? She knew that Mrs Crofton's mind must be dwelling all the time on Laurence, whom she would never see again. He had been filling her own mind during the last three days, but strangely she did not think of him as he had appeared recently but as she had known him years ago. She supposed it was a kindly trick of nature, working against the resentment, which had blotted out the bitterness. Her mind was brought fully back to the proceedings as she felt the movement of John's body: it was as if it had been jerked into awareness. The inspector was addressing him again.

'And how did you deal with the matter, Doctor?'

'I . . . went back to the pool . . .'

All eyes were on John now. He was staring directly at the inspector. His face looked white and drawn and there was an expression in his eyes that frightened Bridget and caused her to exclaim to herself rapidly, Not John! Not John! He would never have done it. Oh, no! And she kept silently repeating, Oh, no! as she listened to him talking.

'Mr Overmeer was at the pool. He was in the cedar hut. He had his gun with him. I spoke to him.'

'Go on, Doctor.' The inspector nodded his head as if in encouragement.

'I spoke to him and I told him not to be a fool. I told him that if he injured Mr Dickenson he would only have to pay for it.'

'What did he say to that?'

'He . . . he told me . . . that he had a good mind to shoot *me*.'

'Yes?'

'We had an exchange of words . . . mostly about our past relationship. I asked him to give me his gun.'

'And what was his reply?'

'He asked me if I wanted one bullet at a time.'

'Go on.'

'I could see it was no use trying to reason with

him; he was very drunk. I . . . left him and made my way towards the east boundary, thinking that I'd meet up with Mr Dickenson coming that way.'

'And you didn't?'

'No.'

'What did you do next?'

'I made for the main road leading to the village, from which branches a lane that leads to Mr Dickenson's farm. I thought that I might meet him there.'

'And you didn't?'

'No, I didn't see Mr Dickenson until after he phoned me and we met outside the gates.'

'And that is your story, Doctor?'

'That is my story.'

'And what did you do after you got into the car, madam?' The question was sprung at Mrs Crofton, bringing her head up. Her lower jaw moved backwards and forwards once or twice before she brought out, 'I . . . I drove straight home.'

'What time did you arrive home?'

'I'm not quite sure.'

'You're not quite sure of anything that happened that night, are you, Mrs Crofton? I would suggest that you didn't go home, that you parked your car somewhere, say up the lane by

Cobber's Wood' – Bridget saw Mrs Crofton's eyes stretching wide and her mouth fall slightly open as she stared at the inspector as he went on quietly, almost unemotionally – 'and then you returned to these grounds and made your way to the pool and the cedar hut.' He paused and rubbed his forehead as if trying to remember something before continuing, 'It's true, isn't it, that you're a very good shot, Mrs Crofton? In the past you and Mr Laurence Overmeer did quite a bit of shooting together?'

There was no movement or murmur from Mrs Crofton.

'Mr Overmeer was shot through the heart with a twelve-bore. He was, we judged, shot from cover at a distance of twenty yards. It would be difficult to take actual aim at this distance through pouring rain unless you were a good shot, don't you agree, Mrs Crofton?'

Bridget saw Mrs Crofton close her eyes; she looked on the point of fainting. She felt John rising from her side and saw Grandma's hand pushed out to check him. At the same time there came from the hall the sound of Sarah Overmeer's voice, and the sound alone startled Bridget, for she hadn't heard or seen her aunt since the night when she had been accused of being the cause of her son's death. She heard her aunt's voice calling now, 'Vance! Vance!' It was unusual for Sarah Overmeer to raise her voice.

The attention of the people in the drawing-room was now divided between Mrs Crofton sitting with bowed head and the commotion close outside the door, but all their heads lifted in the direction of the door when it was thrust open and there stood a man who was a stranger to Bridget. He was tall, over six feet, with delicate, sharp features. He was very smartly dressed, and his whole appearance gave the idea of a businessman.

'Peter!' The name came on a cry from Mrs Crofton.

The inspector now was on his feet and he moved from behind the table, speaking cordially, as if greeting a belated guest. 'Ah, Mr Crofton, come in, come in.' And as he ushered the tall man into the room with one hand he turned to where Sarah and Vance Overmeer stood in the doorway, and taking on an apologetic tone, and in almost a whisper he said, 'The gentleman could be an important witness.' He grasped the door in his hand, waiting to close it upon them, but Sarah Overmeer, with an imperious move-ment of her arm, thrust him aside and walked into the room, her husband following. Immediately, John got to his feet, as did Bridget, and they moved aside to the corner of the room, while Sarah and Vance Overmeer took the vacated seats on the couch. The couch was large enough to hold four, but Bridget knew that her own proximity to her aunt would be unbearable at this time.

The inspector, his expression now slightly pained, as if a magnanimous action of his had been thrown back in his face, turned to where Mrs Crofton was standing now, close to her husband, looking up at him, her face giving full expression to her mental anguish. And this was conveyed again in the exclamation, 'Oh, Peter!' Her head moved desperately on her shoulders as she uttered her husband's name, and the man, looking down at her, but without touching her, said gently, 'Don't worry, Joyce. It had to come. There's an end to everything. Remember you said that yourself; there's an end to everything.'

Bridget stood close against John, her hands folded one on top of the other across her breasts, as if trying to suppress the compassion that she was feeling for these two people, who in this moment were almost oblivious of anyone but themselves. She knew what was to come as clearly as if she had heard it before, and the woman that she now was cried out within her, He wasn't worth it. He wasn't worth all this suffering.

'Would you like to take a seat, Mr Crofton?'

'No, thank you.'

'Will you be seated, Mrs Crofton?'

Mrs Crofton's eyes slowly dropped from her husband's. Her head bowed down to her chest as if held there by a heavy weight, she half-turned from him, groping at the seat he courteously held for her.

'Now, Mr Crofton.' The inspector tapped his fingers together under his chin. 'You have come here because you have something to tell us . . . yes?'

'Yes, I have something to tell you.' The man was looking directly at the inspector. 'I was not speaking the truth last night when I said that I arrived in Durham on the eight-thirty from Doncaster. I arrived on the six-fifteen. When I reached home, my mother, who is staying with me, told me that my wife had gone out earlier.' He stopped here, moistened his lips and seemed about to continue speaking, but his mouth opened and closed and no sound came from it.

The inspector put in quietly, 'And you were surprised, sir, to find your wife out when a severe storm was raging?'

'No. No, I wasn't really surprised.' His words came slowly now and he cast a glance down at his wife's bent head, and the tenderness in the man's face tore at Bridget, and she, too, bowed her head against the sight of such a love. She heard the inspector's voice probing again, drawing the man gently on to the climax that would perhaps lead him to the solution to the mystery. 'And you went out to find your wife, sir?'

'Yes, I did.'

'You knew where to go?'

'Not exactly.'

'But you had an idea?'

'I had an idea.'

'Did you take a gun with you?'

'Yes, I took my gun with me.'

There came to Bridget a deep intake of many breaths. Then the voice went on, 'I came to Balderstone. I was on the drive making my way to the house when I was drawn, as it were, across the garden in the direction of the pool.' The man paused again, and the inspector put in, 'What made you change your mind about coming up to the house?'

'I suppose I saw the futility of it. Armed as I was I wouldn't get anywhere near Mr Overmeer.' He spoke the name in an ordinary tone, as if he was speaking about an ordinary man, who had left no brand on his life.

The inspector put in quickly now, a note of excitement sounding in his voice for the first time, 'You knew then about the pool and the cedar hut?'

'Yes, I had been a guest on a few occasions in this house and had walked in the gardens.'

'That is not what I am meaning, sir.'

'No, I know it is not. But I have no intention of going into details at this moment. I am only going to say briefly that I went within some distance of the pool. I . . . I saw my wife . . .' Here the voice stopped abruptly. Then after a second, continued, 'I saw her talking to Mr Overmeer. I waited until she had moved from him, then I took aim and I shot him. I fired three times. All the bullets found their mark.'

There was a silence in the room, a terrible pain-filled silence; no-one made the slightest movement, no-one attempted to speak. There was not even a sound of breathing now. Bridget was saying to herself, I saw my wife talking with Mr Overmeer. I waited until she moved away. He had not said, I watched them in each other's arms and I waited until they were apart. Oh, the agony that the human mind had to endure!

It was Mr Crofton's voice that broke the stillness in the room. He was speaking to his wife, and again it was as if they were alone. He was looking down at her and she, through the blur of her tears, was gazing up at him as he said,

'There's an end to everything. That's what you said, isn't it, the other evening? There's an end to everything, and I thought there was. I couldn't bear another beginning, Joyce. Don't cry, my dear, don't cry.'

Why had this woman the love of such a man? It wasn't fair, it wasn't fair. He was a good man, a good man, but he would be tried for murder. Oh, the injustice ... the injustice! Bridget's new self was being faced with a picture of life and it was so hurtful and unjust as to be terrifying.

John's arm was around her shoulder, and with his head bent to hers he was whispering, 'Ssh! Don't cry, my dear.'

Groping for her handkerchief, she wiped at her eyes and made an effort to clamp down on her emotion. When she next looked around the room everyone was in a different position. Her grandmother was on her feet and she was standing next to Sarah. Sarah was standing straight and tall, staring to where Mr and Mrs Crofton now stood with the inspector at their side. Perhaps it was the force of her concentrated gaze that brought Mr Crofton round to face her. Bridget watched them looking at each other. There was sorrow in the man's face, but what was the expression on her Aunt Sarah's white face? Bridget was surprised to see there was no hate on it. No look of loathing. If she could put a name to the emotion that she saw it would have been pity, pity for this man who had killed her son. His words rang through Bridget's head again: There's an end to everything. The man had taken all he could stand and Sarah Overmeer recognised this. But her feelings towards his wife would doubtless be different; there would be no pity directed there. Sarah did not look at Mrs Crofton, but turned round slowly and looked at her husband, and Vance Overmeer, with a tenderness that Bridget had never seen him show towards his masterful wife, took her arm and gently led her from the room.

With a glance in Bridget's direction, Hester Gether followed her stepdaughter, and a moment later Kate, Ryder and MacKay also left the room. Bridget saw the inspector now lean forward and say something to Mr Crofton. What it was she could not hear, but in reply Mr Crofton inclined his head slowly. Then, assisting his wife up from the chair with his hand on her elbow, they too left the room, followed by the inspector and his assistant.

From where she stood Bridget saw them walk towards the front door. They looked like a group of friends going home after a visit. A surge of emotion impossible to control swept over her and she covered her face with her hands.

'There now, there now, it's all over.' Her head was pressed into John's shoulder and he was stroking her hair.

'Poor fellow.'

She raised her head as John spoke and he, gazing down at her, said, 'I can't help but say it, but I hope from the bottom of my heart that he gets off scot-free. There'll be a lot in his favour, anyway.'

She swallowed and blinked at him before saying under her breath, 'You may not believe this, but I do too.'

He touched her cheek. 'That's good to know, Bridget.' He was not looking at her but over her head now, and she turned to find Bruce Dickenson standing not more than a few feet from her, and she was overcome by a sense of deep embarrassment.

John relieved her embarrassment by saying, 'Well, Bruce, it's over.'

'Yes, Doctor, it's over, and here's one that's thankful.'

'And count me another.' John slanted his eyes upwards. 'At one time I had a feeling I would never feel free again.'

'Me, too, Doctor. I've never been through

anything like it in me life. And what made it worse for me was the fact that I started it all.'

'No, no, Bruce.' John shook his head emphatically; it was the doctor speaking now. 'Put that idea out of your mind. You were only a very small pawn in the game; it would have happened sooner or later. Perhaps for all concerned,' – he paused and his grip tightened around Bridget's shoulders – 'it's best that it happened sooner. As that poor fellow said, there's got to be an end to everything.'

'It seems hard to me, Doctor.' Bruce's face looked grim now, white and grim. 'I've known Mr Crofton for a good many years. He was a good man, a good father and . . . and too good a husband, I should say. It doesn't seem fair.'

'That's life, Bruce.'

'Aye, it might be, but I don't like the taste of it.'

While Bruce had been talking he had kept his eyes tight on those of John, but now, when there came a lapse in the conversation, he brought his gaze slowly to bear on Bridget and he said simply, 'What can I say?'

The words and tone spoke of his deeply troubled mind, and Bridget, smiling at him, the first smile she had managed for days, said,

'Don't say anything, Bruce. It's all over, everything: forget it.'

'It won't be as easy as that. There's only one thing I want to make clear to you.' He swallowed. 'I understand from the doctor that they are saying,' – he paused – 'that . . . that I did you an injury. I didn't, Bridget. I went mad, but not that mad. I've explained to the doctor.' He flicked his eyes towards John. 'He'll tell you.'

'Please . . . please.' Bridget was shaking her head now, her eyes closed. 'Don't, Bruce. Don't go on, please.'

'All right, I just wanted you to know. Now, I'll away. I won't . . . I won't be seeing you again, Bridget. You'll be leaving soon, I suppose?'

'Yes, as soon as possible.'

'I wish you all the luck in the world, you know that.'

'Yes, I know that, Bruce. And thank you.'

'And you, too, Doctor.'

The two men looked at each other. It was a long look, a secret look that Bridget couldn't fathom. Bruce broke it with a jerk of his head and he turned quickly away and went from the room.

Bridget watched him crossing the hall, and when there came the sound of the front door closing, she turned to John, saying, 'Oh, John, I could cry, and cry, and cry. I feel if I let myself go I'll never stop.'

'Then don't start,' he said caustically. 'Bruce will get over this. And as for Mr Crofton ... judges are not men of iron, they're flesh and blood and they'll weigh all the pros and cons before they pass sentence on a man like him.'

'It isn't only because of them alone that I feel like this, but because of Aunt Sarah's attitude to me ... And then ...' She looked at him, her lashes still wet with her tears. 'Ever since it happened, John, I've had the idea that, well, perhaps it was you.'

'Me who killed Laurence?'

She nodded her head. 'You see, I saw you go out to meet Mrs Crofton that night ... and I saw you leaving by the back staircase the night she came to the house.'

'Oh!'

Again she nodded, and he said, softly, 'And you didn't give me away? Well, the night I went down the back staircase I was trying to waylay Laurence. I wanted to talk to him ... away from the house. Perhaps it's as well I missed him. But ...' He smiled now. 'Never even demanded to know what I was up to? Well, well, you haven't acted a bit like a woman.'

'No, John, I'm afraid I haven't. I think I'm a

failure as a woman.' She turned from him.

'Now come on, come off it.'

'I mean it.'

'You leave others to be a judge of that, miss.' He pulled her round and looked down into her face as he spoke. Then just as quickly he turned from her, saying, 'Come along, let's go and find Grandma. This business will have tried her more than a little. And then we can discuss how soon we can get away later.'

He did not say after the funeral. The funeral that was to take place tomorrow, just a few days before the day on which Laurence should have been married. All the county would be there. People would be sighing with supposed sympathy, while all the time, Bridget knew, their minds would be on the scandal of it all.

If only tomorrow was over and she was away from this house, from the memories that it held. She did not know what kind of life lay before her, except that she was determined that it should be filled with work. From this point of sadness she could not see it containing anything else.

But Bridget did not leave Balderstone the day after the funeral, nor the next day either. A week had passed and she was still in the house, and although the longing to get away was still very much in the forefront of her mind she no longer felt that escape was imperative. She had stayed, because to leave Sarah and Vance Overmeer alone together at this time, would have been a form of cruelty. Both she and her grandmother became of one mind on that.

The funeral over, they had returned to the house, the house that was strangely empty, for as Hester Gether said, Laurence had only been one man, yet his bustling, flamboyant personality had filled the place, and now that he was gone there was left a great emptiness, not for her, or yet for Bridget and certainly not for John, but for Sarah and Vance Overmeer. After all, they were the two main people concerned.

Whether or not the tragedy would bring them together, only time would tell. But it was evident to all who had eyes to see that Vance Overmeer was a changed man and his attitude towards his wife, even in public, was one of tenderness; awkward, perhaps, but nevertheless tenderness. This she accepted calmly, even with indifference an outsider might have been led to think.

After talking the matter over with Bridget and John, it was the old lady who approached Sarah, and putting it as if she were asking a favour, wondered if they could stay on for a few more days.

Sarah's answer was to give her stepmother a long look, then to bow her head.

But now the day had been fixed for their departure. They would leave tomorrow morning. This had been precipitated by John. He insisted he must get back to town and his practice; he had been away long enough, and felt fit to start work again.

Now the old lady and Bridget were sitting before the fire in the study and Bridget was studying her grandmother closely. She had been very quiet for the past half an hour. But quite suddenly Hester Gether raised her head from the book she was supposedly reading and returning Bridget's look, said, 'I have come to a decision, Bridget.'

'That's odd, Grandma, for I have too.'

'You! You have? What kind of decision?' The old lady's voice was curt.

'You tell me yours, then I'll tell you mine.' Bridget smiled as she spoke.

'Well, then.' The old lady rested her head against the back of the chair. 'I have decided to stay on with Sarah for a while. I don't know how long, perhaps as long as she needs me.'

The smile slid from Bridget's face. 'Oh, Grandma!'

'You wouldn't consider staying on here yourself?'

'You want the truth?'

'Of course.'

'No, I couldn't.'

'I knew that before I asked. I have thought it all out, and John agrees with me it would be bad for you.'

'You have talked it over with John?'

'Yes, we have talked it over.'

'And I suppose you've made plans for me?' There was a touch of obstinacy in the tone that brought a smile to the old lady's lips, and she answered, 'No, we haven't, miss; we're going to leave you to make your own. We can offer a few suggestions but that's all. Do you still want to paint?'

'Of course.'

'John thinks you should go to the Slade: your standard is high enough.'

'The Slade?'

'Yes, wouldn't you like that?'

Bridget considered for a moment before saying, 'I don't really know, for it would be like attending school again. I think I would rather freelance and take private lessons. I don't know, Grandma, I'll have to think it over.'

'You do that, and if you decide to go you could live near John.'

'Live near John in that dreadful part of

London?' Bridget scoffed.

'Don't you be so pert, miss. I don't want either of you to live in that dreadful part of London, but if you have to be in London I would rather you were near John.'

'What does he say about that?'

The old lady slowly closed the book on her lap, then leaning slightly forward, she scrutinised Bridget for a moment before saying, 'How do you look upon John?'

'What do you mean, Grandma?'

'Just what I say. How do you look upon him? As a brother? An amusing companion? Someone you can run to in trouble?'

Bridget's eyes narrowed. 'I just don't know, I haven't thought about it much. John has always been there somehow . . . Well, I can't explain.'

'You have. John has always been there. Do you know why John married that nurse?'

'Because he was sorry for her.'

'Yes, he was in a way; he was trying to help her. But he was also trying to help himself, to help himself get over you.'

'Over me?' Bridget's eyes were stretched wide and she repeated, 'Over me?'

'Yes, John has always been in love with you, my dear, and when you were about eighteen he told your Uncle Vance how it was with him. But then Aunt Sarah got to work. I don't want to say anything against Sarah at this moment but you should know this. She knew then that the business was going to need your money, and she also knew that John was very grateful to her for the kindness she had shown him since he came as a boy to this house. She played on this, together with the fact that she knew you were quite silly over Laurence – she knew more than me on that matter. Anyway, she even went as far as to tell John that a marriage had been arranged between you and Laurence but that it was being kept secret for a time, and she swore him to secrecy, too. I'll say this for Laurence, I don't think at that time that he knew anything about his mother's schemes. John himself didn't tell me anything about the arrangement until quite recently. When I was so angry at you for agreeing to marry Laurence, it was then that John told me it had been arranged for years.'

'John!' Bridget cupped her cheek with one hand and repeated, 'John!'

'Is it so hard to believe? Many a woman would thank God on her knees for a man like John to love them.'

'But he's always laughed and joked and never . . . John's always played the clown . . . although not on this last visit.'

'It was a good cover-up, a good façade, but clowns are notoriously sad men underneath, men who feel deeply, who suffer greatly. Now I'll say this to you: if, after this news has soaked in, you don't think that you could ever care for John, then decide to do something that will take you as far out of his way as possible, because there are limits to what a man can put up with.'

'Oh, Grandma!'

'And don't you say, "Oh, Grandma!" like that. But leave that for the moment, and tell me, what was your decision?'

'My decision? Oh!' Bridget jerked her head. What had she decided? Oh, yes, about the money and Uncle Vance. But John ... John in love with her all this time! But why hadn't he shown her that he loved her in that way ...? The new Bridget looked at the shadow of the girl that still clung to her and thought, Don't be silly. If he had, would it have made any difference? Don't forget you have never been able to see anyone else but Laurence; at least, until a few days ago ... What would it be like to spend one's life with John? For answer there came a feeling of warmth round her heart. The numbness that had been in command of her body for days eased slightly.

'Did you hear me? I asked you about this decision of yours.'

'Oh, yes. Well, it's this, Grandma. It's about my money ... How much am I worth altogether?'

'How much are you worth? Well.' The old lady thrust her chin sideways and looked up at the ceiling as if she would find the amount written there. Then, lowering her eyes to meet Bridget's, she exclaimed, 'A hundred thousand, I should say, something like that, all told.'

'It would be a lot of money if I cared anything about money.'

'I've told you before, you would care about it if you hadn't any, believe me you would. And never be so foolish as to despise money.'

'No, Grandma. But at the same time, I don't need a hundred thousand pounds. I would like to help Uncle Vance. I would like to give him what he needs.'

'Hmm! Well, now, we'll have to go into this.' The eyebrows were well up towards the white hair.

'You won't be against it?'

'No ... No, not now. But I have one stipulation. You don't part with all you have; in fact, I would insist on it. Let him borrow half, two-thirds at the most, then if you never recover it you would still have something left.'

'Will you tell Uncle Vance, then?'

'No, I'll do nothing of the sort; it's your money and if you want to give it away you must do the giving yourself. And if you're going to do it I would do it at once. It will at least ease one part of his mind, anyway, and it will definitely be of some solace to your Aunt Sarah to know that, besides all else that has happened to her, she is not going to lose her home. Now come and kiss me and then go and find them.'

As Bridget bent to kiss the wrinkled cheek the old lady said, 'You're a good child, Bridget.' Then quickly contradicting her statement, she added with a sly grin, 'Forgive me, a good girl . . . But let me also tell you, you'll never be a woman until you are married.' And with a push that forbade any retort she sent her towards the door.

The scene with her Uncle Vance and her Aunt Sarah had been so emotionally disturbing that afterwards Bridget felt she must get out of the house and walk. And she walked quickly, not through the garden, but down the drive and out to the main road. She didn't think she would ever again have the courage to go to her once favoured spot, the pool.

Her mind now was filled, to the exclusion of everything else, with sorrow for the two people she had just left. Their almost wordless gratitude – for little had been said when she made her surprising offer – had been unbearable. She saw her Uncle Vance now as a pathetic figure, as a man who had, all his life, been chasing a rainbow and, very like herself a short while ago, someone who had woken up to the fact that you cannot catch rainbows. They are just there to lighten the dark side of life, to make one look up and hope.

Her Aunt Sarah had simply gazed at her, her throat blocked by words she couldn't bring herself to say, but her gratitude was in her eyes and in the tentative touch of her hands as Bridget made to leave the room.

Life was painful. Would it always be like this? No-one seemed to be happy. Bruce Dickenson, Mrs Crofton, that poor man, her husband, her uncle, her aunt, her grandmother. She paused as she came to this name. Her grandmother wasn't unhappy. No, her grandmother wasn't unhappy. And why? Because, she supposed, she was full of courage. She hadn't had an easy life, yet it hadn't made her unhappy. Could courage make you happy?

Then there was John. Was John unhappy? She felt her step slowing. Yes, part of John was unhappy, but he too had the same quality as Grandma; he had courage plus, and the plus was compassion. He never asked for anything for himself. He never would. Someone would have to give him something that he wanted, that he needed but wouldn't take.

She had been amazed at what Grandma had told her. She had always thought, if she thought about it at all, that John's love for her was part of his general love of humanity, perhaps with a little extra thrown in. And, like Bruce Dickenson, he had always treated her as a child.

Could she love John in that way?

She bowed her head before she gave herself an answer, for it seemed irrational to give the question a positive answer, when only two weeks ago she had been in love with Laurence. Her grandmother had said she had never been in love with Laurence, but had been in love with romance. She had been going through the phase of adolescent fantasy. In her case, she had clung on to her adolescence knowing that only by so doing could she keep the fantasy.

But could she love John?

The voice persisted, and she lifted her head from the contemplation of the road and looked away over the fells. Then stepping off the road and onto the heather-covered slopes, she began to walk slowly and steadily. And as she walked she received her answer.

Almost three hours later she returned to the road that led to Balderstone. She was feeling very tired but strangely happy, and not a little excited.

She had been walking on the road only a short while when she heard her name called loudly, and turning, she saw John running towards her from the direction of the village. For every moment of her walk since she had stepped off the road he had been on her mind, and now the sight of him covered her with confusion, but that fled on his greeting: for in a voice unusually harsh, he demanded even before he reached her, 'Where do you think you've been?'

'For a walk.' Her tone was level, her eyes wide.

He stood before her panting. 'Then . . . then why can't you tell people that you're going to walk for hours? Why walk out of the house like that without telling Grandma what you intended to do? She's frantic. Do you know you've been gone almost three hours?'

'Three hours! All that time? No wonder I'm feeling tired.' She found she could smile at his temper.

'You can feel as tired as you like, but I've no sympathy for you. Come on.' He took her by the arm and none too gently, intending to press her forward, but like a mule she did not move her feet from the ground. And when he was forced to remain stationary too, he peered at her, saying, 'What's the matter with you?'

'Nothing, I've just been thinking.'

'Well, is there anything to stop you thinking and walking at the same time?'

'You are in a bad temper, John.'

'Well!' He moved his head from side to side. 'Well, after all the trouble there's been, you suddenly disappear.' His voice was more normal now. 'We searched everywhere ... everywhere ... Down at the pool.' He did not meet her eyes.

'Oh, John, I would not do a thing like that, would I?'

'One doesn't know what people will do, Bridget. And there's been so much happening these last few days. Come, let's get back to Grandma and ease her mind.'

On this she started to walk swiftly along the road, and they had covered some distance in silence before he asked, 'What made you go off like that on your own?'

'Because I wanted to think.' She was looking straight ahead. 'And because I may be a lot on my own in the future.'

'Oh?'

'Grandma suggested I should go to the Slade.'

'Yes, yes, I know that.' He, too, was looking ahead.

'Well, I don't fancy going; it will feel too much like being back to school. But I want to paint . . . yet, strangely, not all the time now. I used to think that was all I wanted to do, just paint every hour of the day. But now I don't think that I'll ever really do anything worthwhile in that line. I shall always like painting; it will give me pleasure, but I can't see me competing with Rembrandt.' She smiled as she looked at him, but he was still gazing ahead. He was, she realised, not going to help her in any way, and again they walked in silence.

'Grandma says it will be better to live near you than on my own in Chelsea . . . or some such place.'

Her words caused him to falter, and he glanced at her quickly. 'When did she say that?'

'Oh . . . this morning when we were talking—'

'You were talking about going to London?'

'Yes, she thinks it would be a good idea.'

'Oh, does she?' He was nodding his head as if at the distant gates of the house.

'Wouldn't you like me to live near you?'

'That's quite beside the point. It's a poor district, as Grandma has so often pointed out. You would soon get very tired of looking out on brick walls all the time, not to mention gangs of grimy children cluttering your front door.'

'You forget that I know what the district is like.'

'I forget nothing. You have passed through it. At most you have spent a few hours in it.'

Her lips were slightly apart now, smiling as she said, 'I could always leave if I didn't like it.' His head jerked towards her again, and he held her eyes before looking away and saying, 'Yes, you could always leave, that's true, but I'm there for life.'

'You needn't be; you could move, get a better practice.'

He had stopped dead and brought her to a halt. Again he stared at her for some time, before he said, 'I'm there for life, Bridget; I know what I have to do and I can do it better among those people. I'm not playing the philanthropist. I like doctoring and I like doctoring where it is most needed, so I won't be moving away.'

'Not even for me, John?' Her words were scarcely audible.

'Bridget! What has Grandma been saying?'

'Oh, lots of things . . . opening my eyes.'

'She had no right to. And look, Bridget,' – his voice was unsteady – 'don't see yourself as any dewy-eyed Florence Nightingale helping me out in my practice. There are too many experienced women doing social work around there.'

She would not allow herself to be rebuffed by the assertion, for she knew what he was trying to do. She said, 'I could never see myself in that capacity; I'm terrified of blood, anyway. But . . .' Could she go on and say it? Could she say something that he wanted to say but wouldn't allow himself to? She remembered thinking earlier that he was always doing something for someone else and it was time that someone did something for him. She forced herself to look into the deep brown eyes as she said, 'I can't see myself ever as a Florence Nightingale, or any doctor's right hand, but . . . but I have the idea that I'd like to be in a doctor's house some day, and running it.'

Now she could no longer look into his eyes, for the brown had almost deepened into black; in their depths was a shining light. 'Bridget!' He had hold of her hands. 'You are just saying this because you are unhappy.'

'No, no, John.'

'In a few months' time you will regret being so impetuous.'

She still kept her eyes cast downwards. 'Try me. Let me live near you and work . . . at my painting and anything else that turns up, except . . . Florence Nightingaling.'

'Oh, Bridget . . . Bridget.' They were laughing now, standing in the centre of the road, their arms around each other, her head pressed tight into his neck. His hand running through her hair, he muttered incoherently, 'Oh, there's so much I want to say, so much I want to tell you. Since you were a little child I've . . . oh, I've adored you, Bridget. I've . . . Oh, let it rest. If I start I'll never stop telling you about a little girl called Bridget Gether . . . What is it? Oh, Bridget!' He lifted her face from his shoulder. 'Don't cry. Now, now. Don't. Come on, I'm not going to have you crying, not at this moment . . . Look at me, Bridget.' She looked at him as he said solemnly, 'I'll make you happy, Bridget. I'll make you so happy you won't see the bricks and mortar, nor the dirty kids.'

'Do you ever think of yourself, John?'

'All the time.'

'Oh, John.' She hesitated. 'There's something else I . . . I'd better tell you . . . I've given over most of my money to Uncle Vance.'

'Good. Now we can start even.' He cupped her face in his hands. 'I'm glad you did that,

Bridget; it was a great gesture. Uncle Vance will still have his work, and Aunt Sarah her home. It won't be everything but it will be something for them to hang on to. And now we'd better hurry back to Balderstone, if I don't want to examine one Hester Gether, who had just died from worry because she couldn't find her grand-daughter.' He gripped her hand as if he was about to run with her up the road, yet neither of them moved. Their faces were close, although his remained still. It was Bridget who, leaning forward, placed her lips on his. It was a gentle kiss, a promise, and as such he received it. And so warm and tender was the light in his eyes, so deep was the light of love in them for her that she knew with a surge of exhilarating certainty that life with this man would be good, even wonderful.

They walked on up the road, their hands joined, a man and a girl who was now on the way to becoming a woman.

THE END

JUSTICE IS A WOMAN
by Catherine Cookson

The day Joe Remington brought his new bride to
Fell Rise, he had already sensed she might not
settle easily into the big house just outside the
Tyneside town of Fellburn. For Joe this had
always been his home, but for Elaine it was
virtually another country whose manners and
customs she was by no means eager to accept.

Making plain her disapproval of Joe's familiarity
with the servants, demanding to see accounts Joe
had always trusted to their care, questioning the
donation of food to striking miners' families – all
these objections and more soon rubbed Joe and
the local people up the wrong way, a problem he
could easily have done without, for this was
1926, the year of the General Strike, the effects of
which would nowhere be felt more acutely than
in this heartland of the North-East.

Then when Elaine became pregnant, she saw it
as a disaster and only the willingness of her
unmarried sister Betty to come and see her
through her confinement made it bearable. But in
the long run, would Betty's presence only serve to
widen the rift between husband and wife, or
would she help to bring about a reconciliation?

0 552 13622 0

THE MALTESE ANGEL
by Catherine Cookson

Ward Gibson knew exactly what was expected of
him by the village folk, and especially by the
Mason family, whose daughter Daisy he had
known all his life. But then, in a single week, his
whole world had been turned upside down by a
dancer, Stephanie McQueen, who seemed to float
across the stage of the Empire Music Hall where
she was appearing as The Maltese Angel. To his
amazement, the attraction was mutual, and after
a whirlwind courtship she agreed to marry him.

But a scorpion had already begun to emerge
from beneath the stone of the local community,
who considered that Ward had betrayed their
expectations, and had led on and cruelly deserted
Daisy. There followed a series of reprisals on his
family, one of them serious enough to cause him
to exact a terrible revenge; and these events
would twist and turn the course of many lives
through Ward's own and succeeding generations.

0 552 13684 0

PURE AS THE LILY
by Catherine Cookson

Mary Walton was the apple of her da's eye. For
long now he had been out of work, and Mary
was his only comfort during those dark years of
the Depression, when unemployment and a
nagging, ambitious wife gnawed away at his
self-respect. Once he was a man who had held his
head high with Geordie pride; now his only hope
was that Mary would escape from the grinding
poverty of the Tyneside slums that had held him a
prisoner for so many years.

But then something happened to Mary that
shattered all his dreams of her future – an event
that was to split a family and influence its
members for generations to follow...

0 552 14073 2

THE YEAR OF THE VIRGINS
by Catherine Cookson

It had never been the best of marriages and over recent years it had become effectively a marriage in name and outward appearance only. Yet, in the autumn of 1960, Winifred and Daniel Coulson presented an acceptable façade to the outside world, for Daniel had prospered sufficiently to allow them to live at Wearcill House, a mansion situated in the most favoured outskirt of the Tyneside town of Fellburn.

Of their children, it was Donald on whom Winifred doted to the point of obsession, and now he was to be married, Winifred's prime concern was whether Donald was entering wedlock with an unbesmirched purity of body and spirit, for amidst the strange workings of her mind much earlier conceptions of morality and the teachings of the church held sway.

There was something potentially explosive just below the surface of life at Wearcill House, but when that explosion came it was in a totally unforeseeable and devastating form, plunging the Coulsons into an excoriating series of crises out of which would come both good and evil, as well as the true significance of the year of the virgins.

'The power and mastery are astonishing'
Elizabeth Buchan, *Sunday Times*

0 552 13247 0

THE GOLDEN STRAW
by Catherine Cookson

The Golden Straw, as it would be named, was a large, broad-brimmed hat presented to Emily Pearson by her long-time friend and employer Mabel Arkwright, milliner and modiste. And before long it was to her employer that Emily owed the gift of the business itself, for Mabel was in poor health and had come to rely more and more on Emily before her untimely death in 1880.

While on holiday in France, Emily and the Golden Straw attracted the eye of Paul Steerman, a guest at the hotel, and throughout his stay he paid her unceasing attention. But Paul Steerman was not all he seemed to be and he was to bring nothing but disgrace and tragedy to Emily, precipitating a series of events that would influence the destiny of not only her children but her grandchildren too.

The Golden Straw, conceived on a panoramic scale, brilliantly portrays a rich vein of English life from the heyday of the Victorian era to the stormy middle years of the present century. It represents a fresh triumph for this great storyteller whose work is deservedly loved and enjoyed throughout the world.

0 552 13685 9

A DINNER OF HERBS
by Catherine Cookson

A legacy of hatred can be a terrible force in life, over which not even an enduring love and all the fruits of material success may prevail. Catherine Cookson explores this theme in a major novel that will absorb and enthral her readers as irresistibly as any she has written.

Roddy Greenbank was brought by his father to the remote Northumberland community of Langley in the autumn of 1807. Within hours of their arrival, however, the father had met a violent death, and the boy left with all memory gone of his past life.

Adopted and raised by old Kate Makepeace, Roddy found his closest companions in Hal Royston and Mary Ellen Lee. These three stand at the heart of a richly eventful narrative that spans the first half of the nineteenth century, their lives lastingly intertwined by the inexorable demands of a strange and somewhat cruel destiny.

0 552 12551 2

A SELECTION OF OTHER CATHERINE COOKSON TITLES AVAILABLE FROM CORGI BOOKS

THE PRICES SHOWN BELOW WERE CORRECT AT THE TIME OF GOING TO PRESS. HOWEVER TRANSWORLD PUBLISHERS RESERVE THE RIGHT TO SHOW NEW RETAIL PRICES ON COVERS WHICH MAY DIFFER FROM THOSE PREVIOUSLY ADVERTISED IN THE TEXT OR ELSEWHERE.

13576 3	THE BLACK CANDLE	£6.99
12473 7	THE BLACK VELVET GOWN	£5.99
14633 1	COLOUR BLIND	£5.99
12551 2	A DINNER OF HERBS	£6.99
14066 X	THE DWELLING PLACE	£5.99
14068 6	FEATHERS IN THE FIRE	£5.99
14089 9	THE FEN TIGER	£5.99
14069 4	FENWICK HOUSES	£5.99
10450 7	THE GAMBLING MAN	£4.99
13716 2	THE GARMENT	£5.99
13621 2	THE GILLYVORS	£5.99
14468 1	THE GIRL	£5.99
14328 6	THE GLASS VIRGIN	£5.99
13685 9	THE GOLDEN STRAW	£5.99
13300 0	THE HARROGATE SECRET	£5.99
14087 2	HERITAGE OF FOLLY	£5.99
13303 5	THE HOUSE OF WOMEN	£5.99
10780 8	THE IRON FAÇADE	£5.99
13622 0	JUSTICE IS A WOMAN	£5.99
14091 0	KATE HANNIGAN	£5.99
14092 9	KATIE MULHOLLAND	£5.99
14081 3	MAGGIE ROWAN	£5.99
13684 0	THE MALTESE ANGEL	£5.99
10321 7	MISS MARTHA MARY CRAWFORD	£5.99
12524 5	THE MOTH	£5.99
13302 7	MY BELOVED SON	£5.99
13088 5	THE PARSON'S DAUGHTER	£5.99
14073 2	PURE AS THE LILY	£5.99
13683 2	THE RAG NYMPH	£5.99
14620 X	THE ROUND TOWER	£5.99
13714 6	SLINKY JANE	£5.99
10541 4	THE SLOW AWAKENING	£5.99
10630 5	THE TIDE OF LIFE	£5.99
14038 4	THE TINKER'S GIRL	£5.99
12368 4	THE WHIP	£5.99
13577 1	THE WINGLESS BIRD	£5.99
13247 0	THE YEAR OF THE VIRGINS	£5.99

All Transworld titles are available by post from:
Book Service By Post, PO Box 29, Douglas, Isle of Man, IM99 1BQ
Credit cards accepted. Please telephone 01624 675137,
fax 01624 670923, Internet http://www.bookpost.co.uk
or e-mail: bookshop@enterprise.net for details.
Free postage and packing in the UK. Overseas customers: allow
£1 per book (paperbacks) and £3 per book (hardbacks).